A MURDER IN TIME

by

Jonas Saul

PUBLISHED BY:
Imagine Press Inc.
Amazon Paperback ISBN: 979-8-689607-46-7
Ebook ISBN: 978-1-927404-31-7
Hardcover ISBN: 978-1-998047-81-9

A Murder in Time
Copyright © 2014 by Jonas Saul

The Sarah Roberts Series

Dark Visions (One)
The Warning (Two)
The Crypt (Three)
The Hostage (Four)
The Victim (Five)
The Enigma (Six)
The Vigilante (Seven)
The Rogue (Eight)
Killing Sarah (Nine)
The Antagonist (Ten)
The Redeemed (Eleven)
The Haunted (Twelve)
The Unlucky (Thirteen)
The Abandoned (Fourteen)
The Cartel (Fifteen)
Losing Sarah (Sixteen)
The Pact (Seventeen)
The Terror (Eighteen)
The Chase (Nineteen)
The Betrayal (Twenty)
Sarah's Return (Twenty-One)
The Hunt (Twenty-Two)
The Delivery (Twenty-Three)
The Trap (Twenty-Four)
The Ultimatum (Twenty-Five)
The Depraved (Twenty-Six)
The Condemned (Twenty-Seven)
Payback (Twenty-Eight)
The Unknown (Twenty-Nine)
Wrath (Thirty)
The Damned (Thirty-One)
The Game (Thirty-Two)
The Decoy (Thirty-Three)
The Disappearance (Thirty-Four)
The Whole Truth (Thirty-Five)
Alex (Thirty-Six)
Parkman (Thirty-Seven)
Darwin (Thirty-Eight)

Aaron (Thirty-Nine)
Remains To Be Seen (Forty)

The Jake Wood Novels

The Immortal Gene (Book One)
The Immortal Target (Book Two)

Standalone Novels

'Til Death Do Us Part
The Drowning
The Woman in the Woods
The Threat
The Specter
The Mafia Trilogy
A Murder in Time
Frequency of the Dead

Co-Authored Novels

Collision Course (Written with Gary Ponzo)
There Will Be Blood (Written with Rania Stone)
The Soulless (Written with Rania Stone)

Short Story Collections

Twisted Fate (Tales of Horror)
Twists of Fate (Tales of Hope)

Chapter 1

THE ONLY WAY MARCUS Johnson could get any serious cash would be to steal it. Once the money was stashed in his car, he would call the police on himself.

It was the only way he could pull it off.

His was the perfect plan.

Why stay legal? Why do anything good when the rewards aren't there?

He had worked too long and hard for his boss, Frankie, to not get a little something on the side. Marcus had built Frankie's business from day one when no one was coming through the door. Now Frankie's store, The Act of Love, was doing over a thousand bucks a day. All Marcus had ever gotten was a small raise six months ago and a tin of Treasures of the Sea Kama Sutra bathing salts for his girlfriend, Katy.

Enough was enough.

Marcus was entitled to something bigger, better. It was his time to get paid, and Frankie could do nothing about it.

No one would get hurt. In fact, no one would ever know it was him. Except maybe his mother, God rest her soul. She had died when he was eight years old. He was sure she was watching from above, but who would she tell?

The theft of a few thousand dollars would only matter when he followed her to the great prize in the sky. Down here, where money ruled everything, stealing it was the only way.

He locked the front door to the store and cut the lights. At the window, he stared across the expanse of the empty parking lot to watch the cars pass by on the road. A hefty biker rode by slowly on a Harley Davidson, turning to examine the mannequins in the store window.

Marcus's boss, Frankie, was at a trade show in Los Angeles tonight and wouldn't be back until Tuesday morning. It had been a quiet Sunday, and most of the stores in the strip mall had closed hours ago.

The biker guided his Harley through the empty parking lot to the street, turned right, and drove away. Marcus watched it leave, his stomach churning with the knowledge of what he was about to do.

Something moved in the parking lot by a light standard. He squinted and leaned closer to the glass.

A man in a T-shirt and jeans stood, partially hidden, watching the front of the store. From this distance, it looked like the man was watching him, but it was hard to tell as half his body was still behind the large base of the light's thick pole.

The man wiped at his eyes.

Is he crying?

Marcus nodded to see if the guy would respond.

Instead, the man turned away and half jogged, half walked toward the road. The man's feet were bare. After a quick glance over his shoulder toward the store, the man increased his speed to a run and disappeared in the shadows by the road.

Weird.

Marcus turned around and moved toward the counter. There was something familiar about the man in the parking lot. It nagged at him as he prepared to close out his till. Something as familiar as family.

He shrugged off the creepy feeling and eyed each of the three cameras in the front of the store as he stepped behind the counter to finish the closing procedures.

A quad camera system covered the counter and each wall running the length of the store. The fourth camera surveyed the back door. If he was going to pull this off, he had to act normal because the police would yank the camera feed by the morning, and he would be in jail before lunch tomorrow if he showed them any reason to suspect him.

Acting was his gig. Marcus could lie with a straight face and convince anybody of the fabricated truth. Only Katy could see through him. But with enough emotion, he was sure he could win her over, too.

His beloved Katy. What would she think if she knew what he was about to do? He had no choice, though. He had walled himself into a financial box that had cost more than expected. The promises he had made to Katy required money, and he would do anything for her, which meant keeping his promises. If he got caught, he would serve his time, but he wouldn't get caught.

Anything for Katy.

Samuel Levy and his support group would be pissed. The Early Onset Neighborly Support Group wouldn't condone this sort of thing, so he could never tell any of them. It was without question that he wouldn't be discussing any of this at his next meeting because Samuel Levy, his best friend since they met at the bi-weekly meeting a few months back, would vilify him if he found out what Marcus was up to.

No one would ever know it was Marcus who robbed the store. Not if he had anything to do with it.

He was staring off into space, thinking, when he blinked out of it. He had to keep moving.

The cameras.

He shook off the nerves, picked up a pen, and recorded the computer's numbers onto the cash-out sheet. Once the sheet was totaled, he stapled everything together, backed the computer up to the online Dropbox, and turned it off. Then he closed the Interac machine, or as Frankie called it, the POS terminal, and balanced the totals against the cash-out sheet.

Do everything normal, then call the police.

It felt like a two-year-old Duracell battery was dissolving in the enzymes of his stomach. There was no turning back, though. He wouldn't talk himself out of this. He deserved it, and so did Katy.

Once it was done, he could take Katy to dinner and the theater in Toronto he had promised her. He could buy her that ring they had looked at. She would finally feel how much he loved and needed her.

She was his last chance at a life. He had just turned twenty-eight, and Katy Webster was his salvation and final destination. He would be dead by the time he was in his mid-thirties, and even knowing that Katy willingly loved him back.

There was no greater treasure than love. It's so great, many fear it, but Marcus didn't. At least not anymore.

He would have to be careful with the money. Wait until the next payday to announce that he'd been saving for some time and was ready to take the next step. It would devastate him if she suspected he had anything to do with the robbery.

At the back of the store, outside the eye of the fourth camera's range, he slipped on a pair of gloves. This was the moment he dreaded, the point of no return. Once he pried the company safe open with the crowbar, there would be no way to explain it other than the plan he had formulated.

The phone rang.

He jolted as if stung by electricity and grabbed the counter.

Who would call the store twenty minutes after closing on a Sunday night?

His stomach rolled. Sweat beaded on his forehead. His hands shook, and his heart rate increased his breathing.

Could it be Frankie? What would he want?

It rang again.

He considered not answering it. Let it go to the company's answering machine. But the cameras would clock him in at this time, so he had to pick it up.

Act normal.

He grabbed the phone on the third ring.

"The Act of Love. How can I help you?"

"Marcus …"

Oh, shit.

"Dad, are you drunk again?"

"Marcus, we have to talk."

He moved the phone to the other ear and leaned against the counter, taking a moment to calm down and breathe.

"What do we have to talk about this time?" Marcus asked.

"Your mother."

This surprised him. He looked up at the far wall and stared at nothing.

"Why, Dad? What does Mom have to do with anything? She's been dead twenty years now."

"I have to tell you the truth."

Marcus pushed off the counter and paced the carpet under camera four. His father usually brought up the truth when he was drunk. The truth about science. The truth about the government. The truth about women.

The truth is you're a broken-down drunk.

"Tell me, what's the truth about Mom?"

"She did amazing things, and some of them were horrible."

"Really? Amazing and horrible?"

"Yes, Son. Just come and see me. I'll explain everything. You'll finally hear the truth."

"Like the last time at Christmas? When I brought Katy over, you embarrassed me with the truth about my childhood. Stories of me running around the house, disappearing, and reappearing in different bedrooms. You were so drunk you didn't even know we called that game hide and go seek."

His father fell silent. After the words left his mouth, Marcus immediately regretted them. He didn't want to hurt his already clinically depressed drunk of a father, but sometimes *he* needed to hear the truth.

The distinctive sounds of swallowing came through the receiver as his father chugged back whatever poison he had at his disposal.

"Dad? You still there?"

"Yeah—" He hiccupped. "Just come see me. I have something for you that'll explain everything."

"Okay, Dad. Soon."

He had to get his head back in the game. He had gone too far to turn back now. Friday, Saturday, and Sunday's cash adding up to over two thousand dollars sat in the safe waiting for him.

He was about to hang up, but his dad said something else.

"What was that?" Marcus asked.

"Have you ever seen yourself lately?"

He frowned and looked at the phone in his hand, thinking about the familiar guy in the parking lot from five minutes ago who appeared to be watching the front of the store. When he placed the phone back against his ear, he asked, "What are you talking about? Like in a mirror?"

"No, bumped into yourself on the street."

"You mean like a doppelgänger? A body double?"

"No." He breathed in deeply over the phone. "I mean, you. Have you seen you?"

"You're not making sense, Dad. Look, I'm closing up shop and … wait. I just heard something outside."

An idea came to him at that moment. Since his father called him and can testify that someone was at the back door, it would make his story even more believable.

"Look, Dad, it's Sunday night. I have to finish closing the store and get home to Katy, and now I have to check who's at the back door."

"Come see me," his father said and hung up.

Marcus set the phone down. It had become so hard to talk to his father in recent years. Dad was all the family he had left. No brothers, no sisters, and a memory for a mother. Katy was family, but dad was blood.

If only he'd stop drinking.

Marcus picked up the crowbar.

The cameras fed into a monitor in Frankie's office. Marcus had seen the area each camera covered dozens of times and memorized it exactly. The back camera covered no more than eight feet on either side of the back door. Standing near the safe with the crowbar in hand, he was still at least five feet from the camera's view.

He bent on one knee, slipped the end of the crowbar into the crack at the top of the safe's small door, and applied pressure. The door was stronger than he thought. He had to get his body weight into it. He leaned harder on the end of the crowbar.

His forehead moistened, then collected and dripped sweat into his eyes. His hands slipped inside the gloves. He yanked and pried until his face flushed red, and he was breathing hard.

The safe's door had bent back enough to slip a pen through the hole. He needed to get his hand in there. If he didn't get the money, it was all for nothing.

He had to get to the cash inside.

Dealing with the police and everything else would be pointless if the cash weren't his.

In frustration, he jabbed the end of the crowbar into the front of the safe five times, shouting on the last two jabs. The world spun for a moment, then cleared.

He lay down on the cold floor and stared at the ceiling to contemplate his predicament. What if he couldn't get to the cash? What if the crowbar just wasn't good enough? Maybe he could get a wire hanger out of the employee closet, bend it until it was relatively straight, apply something sticky to the end like gum, then slip it inside the safe and pull the Ziploc-wrapped money up through the small hole the employees dropped the packages down.

That wouldn't work. He didn't have any gum. He couldn't afford the delay of leaving to get some.

Maybe this is the stupidest idea I've ever had.

He rolled over, got to his knees, inserted the crowbar tip into the small hole he'd already created, and started again. He continued his assault on the safe for a full five minutes before seeing any progress. It was getting late. If he didn't finish this soon, he was done for.

He checked the size of the hole by pushing his hand inside. It almost cleared his knuckles. Just a little more coaxing, and he could reach inside to retrieve the cash.

Then his cell phone rang.

He scrambled to his feet and looked at the screen.

Katy.

He started to answer, then stopped. If the store were being robbed, he wouldn't be allowed to answer his phone. He whispered a silent apology to his future wife and got back on his knees to finish working on the safe. The phone quieted.

After a few minutes, he could get his entire hand through the hole. He tossed the crowbar aside and pushed his hand in past the wrist, along the forearm, and down toward the bottom of the safe until his fingers came in contact with the supple Ziploc bags.

He squeezed one with his fingers and brought it up and out.

Two hundred and fifty dollars.

The money from his shift never made it into the locked safe, so that made his total so far add up to $940.00.

He reached in again and pulled another. Four hundred and twenty from yesterday afternoon.

He did this again and again until the safe was empty. Then he collected all the tiny baggies and stuffed them into his pockets.

Back on his feet, he collected the two full garbage bags he had placed by the back door, slipped into his jacket, and opened the door to a clear night. A soft breeze caressed him as he carried the two bags toward the garbage bin.

Both bins were surrounded by a structure that resembled a small wooden house for cosmetic reasons. The gate in front of the bins was locked. Marcus set the bags down, pulled out the key, and took a final look around. On a Sunday night, through closing at this hour for the past two years, Marcus knew how quiet it would be. Barely the sound of a single car could be heard over the silence of the evening since Frankie's store was partially located in an industrial area of Toronto just off Keele Street North.

He slipped the key in the lock, clicked it open, and let go of the mechanism.

Then he left the garbage bin and the two bags on the ground and ran to his car, parked in the front of the store. He pulled the cash out of his pockets and stashed it under the driver's seat in a tennis ball container he had placed there for this purpose. Then he closed and locked his car and headed for the store's back door.

Damn, the gloves.

He slipped them off and opened his car again to toss them in. After shutting the door, he reopened it in frustration, grabbed the gloves off the seat, and threw them on the floor by the tennis ball container. He couldn't leave them out in the open if investigating officers peeked into his car.

Finally, once again, he locked his car and headed around the building to the garbage bin. Once there, he pulled out a switchblade knife and applied the tip to his cheek.

The final act has commenced.

With long strides, he walked to the back door of the store, applying pressure to the skin of his cheek with the knife as he went.

He walked up the stairs, stopped at the back door, and gathered the nerve to cut himself. Without thinking about it further, he pushed the knife through his skin as if slicing the skin of a tomato with a deep grunt. Moaning the entire time, he sliced along the cheekbone until the tip hit his jaw, where he pulled the knife out. Blood rushed over the tip of the knife and down his hand. Blood quickly covered his neck.

He wondered if he had done more damage than he intended. Could he pass out before he finished what he needed to do?

He threw the knife as hard as he could into the bushes that ran along the back of the store. He would retrieve the knife and destroy it as soon as he could. This was a simple robbery. The police didn't have the kind of budget to dispatch a search team for the weapon. A murder case, yes, but not the robbery of an adult store. There probably wouldn't even be an investigation.

He ran inside the store and headed for Frankie's office. Once there, he body checked the locked door. It took three hits to buckle it in far enough to kick at the handle.

After snapping it open, he ran over to the cameras and flicked the power bar off, cutting their electrical source. The monitor went blank, and the quad coverage ceased.

In the back room, he picked up his cell phone and lay on the floor, waiting for the pain in his face to subside, but it only seemed to worsen. The hard part was when he grimaced at the pain, which moved his now flabby cheek skin, adding what felt like a hundred bee stings of pain.

He moaned under his breath and closed his eyes as blood leaked from his right cheek.

I've done it, but have I gone too far?

He opened his eyes. It felt like an hour had passed.

His cell phone was ringing.

Weakened, he lifted the phone. Katy.

He answered it.

"Baby …" he whispered.

"Marcus, where are you?" Katy asked. "You should have been home hours ago."

"Honey …" He moaned the word, keeping his lips still.

"What's wrong?" she asked. "Why are you talking like that?"

"Call … police."

He clicked the end button, lowered his hand, and passed out.

Chapter 2

KATY GAVE THE PARAMEDICS room to tend to Marcus. She covered her emotions well for Marcus but couldn't help worrying about what might have been. Whoever robbed the store could have killed him. Even though they cut his face, she felt that was small compared to what they could have done.

One of the attendants stuck his head out the back of the ambulance and addressed the two officers who stood close, waiting to have a word with Marcus. "Officers, we'll have to take him to the hospital to be stitched up properly. He can't give a statement in this condition as any movement of his mouth is quite painful."

"Understood," the taller officer said. "We'll follow and meet you at the hospital."

"I need to go with him," Katy interjected.

The paramedic waved for her to jump up, and he shut the door behind her. Then he walked to the front, where the other paramedic got the ambulance underway.

Katy sat beside Marcus and held his hand gingerly. She entwined her fingers with his and squeezed softly. His eyes fluttered open.

She smiled down at him, her eyes filled with tears.

"Marcus," she whispered.

He tried to smile but caught himself and stopped.

"Oh, baby," Katy said. "I'm so happy you're okay."

"Ee oo."

"Did you say, 'me too'?"

He nodded, his head barely moving. His tongue eased out of his mouth and wet his lips. Then he said something indiscernible. She leaned closer, placing her ear above his mouth.

"There were two of them," he mumbled.

"Marcus, not now," Katy said as she leaned away to look at him. "Wait for the police. I'm just so happy you're alive."

More tears ran down her cheeks. He closed his eyes.

It didn't take long before the ambulance stopped and the back doors opened. Katy hopped out, and the paramedics pulled Marcus to the edge, where the stretcher's wheels folded down to meet the concrete. Then they pushed him through the emergency doors. She followed as far as she could and then detoured to the hospital cafeteria. It was almost three in the morning, and she wanted a coffee.

The cops had been thorough and fast. Before Marcus was in the ambulance, it sounded like they had figured almost everything out. Katy overheard them deduce that Marcus probably jumped while taking the garbage out, held at knifepoint as the safe was broken into.

Someone had turned off the cameras in the locked office. That was something they wanted Marcus to answer. Katy overheard one cop ask the other how the robbers knew where to look for the cameras.

As if Marcus would be a party to this robbery, she thought.

There was a simple answer. They had demanded Marcus tell them where the cameras fed to, and the knife in the cheek would have persuaded him to answer.

But the police always suspected the people closest to the crime before they worked their way outward by the process of elimination.

Katy knew this and was okay with it. There was no way Marcus Johnson was part of a robbery of the store where he had worked for more than two years. Especially after how well Frankie had treated him. No way. Marcus and Frankie were like brothers.

She poured a coffee from the self-serve counter, inhaled coffee fumes through her nose, and closed her eyes. It brought her back to when she had met Marcus at a Starbucks. When he spilled his coffee across his lap after allowing his gaze to linger on her too long, she had grabbed a towel from the clerk and helped Marcus clean it up. They chatted and agreed to meet for coffee again, but he decided to not wear it the next time.

She had called him Hot Pants for a while after that. It wasn't until she had fallen for him that he trusted her enough to tell her about his condition.

He had the gene that causes Early Onset Familial Alzheimer's Disease, which usually affected people fifty or older, but some as early as sixteen.

His mother had died in a car accident when she was thirty-eight, just as her Alzheimer's symptoms had started.

When he was twenty-six, Marcus warned Katy two years ago that he had anywhere from five to ten good years left before Alzheimer's would set in.

They had tested for the gene and found it. Doctors told him he had a genetic predisposition because the gene was passed to him from a first-degree relative who had it, namely his mother. Marcus was told there was zero chance of escaping his fate.

Knowing all that, he lived life with a zany approach, searching for fun ways to make her smile and enrich her life beyond her wildest dreams. No man had ever made her this happy. She smiled at his antics and hoped this experience didn't change him. She had grown to love Marcus for whom he was.

After paying a sleepy-looking cafeteria employee for the coffee, she wandered the hospital halls until she made it to admitting in emergency. They directed her to a small cubicle where they were about to suture up Marcus's face.

His eyes were open, a large white bandage covering his cheek. He tried to smile when she stepped in.

"Don't," she said. "It's okay. I'm just happy you're okay."

"I'm no hero," he mumbled without moving his lips. "I didn't even fight back."

"You're my hero." She set what was left of her coffee on a small table by the head of the bed and moved closer to him. "What happened tonight? How much can you tell me without moving your face?"

"Two guys."

She nodded and leaned closer.

"Behind the garbage bin. Jumped me. Knifed me. Made me turn the cameras off. Brought a crowbar with them. I think they took the money from the safe. Not sure because they kept me by the door, and then you called."

She met his gaze. "I'm so sorry you had to go through that. Did you get a look at them? Can you identify them?"

He rolled his head back and forth on the white pillow. "Balaclavas."

"This sucks for Frankie, too. You know his temper."

"I know. I feel bad. The whole weekend's receipts. He wasn't around to do the banking."

"Yeah, I'd say he's gonna be pissed."

"You sticking around?" Marcus asked.

"Of course. I'm driving you home when they're done."

"I'd smile." He swallowed hard. "But hurts too much. I'll smile later."

She patted his shoulder. "I'll be waiting outside."

She grabbed her coffee cup, turned around, and almost bumped into two police officers stepping inside the small cubicle.

"Our turn," the tall one said.

"You okay to do this?" Katy asked Marcus.

He nodded.

She headed for the waiting lounge area, not liking the look of either cop one bit.

Chapter 3

THOUGH NERVOUSNESS AND THE subtle pain in Marcus's face were causing him to feel squeamish, the irritation at how the officers entered really pissed him off. They had almost bumped into Katy and then said it was their turn as if they were tag-teaming him.

The tall officer scowled. The shorter cop appeared friendly and cordial, like a nice teacher about to tell him he had passed the final exam.

"Can you talk?" the friendly one asked. "Your mouth okay?"

"Yeah," Marcus said. "Just can't move my lips much."

"Fair enough."

Both men pulled pads and pens out in unison as if rehearsed. He wondered why they would both have to write the same information. Couldn't one write and the other ask the questions?

"Can you state your name, age, and date of birth?"

Marcus told them and then repeated the same story he had told Katy, word for word, as both officers wrote furiously.

"And you didn't get a look at either one?"

"No."

"Voices. Recognize them?"

"No."

"Who pulled the power on the cameras?"

"I did," he said without hesitation.

The officers exchanged a glance. Then the tall one stepped closer to the bed, his scowl changed to a serious frown.

"Why would you do that?"

"They told me to."

"Oh yeah," he said with a laugh, clearly mocking Marcus. "We do things people tell us to all the time."

They didn't believe his story. He could tell that right away. Or they were questioning him while making him think they suspected him. He had to think and act as if someone had jumped him. Pretend in his mind that that actually happened and respond in kind.

"They had a knife to my face," Marcus said, without blinking, staring down the angrier cop.

"As you said," the tall one replied, his frown lifting. "Explain how these two bad guys even knew there was a camera system monitoring the back of the store."

He hadn't thought of that. But he couldn't let them see him falter.

"Maybe they looked up at the ceiling before entering the store," he said too fast.

"You're saying these guys took the time to examine the ceiling for cameras?"

"Yeah. Must've."

Marcus realized neither officer had offered him their names or identified themselves.

The tall one flipped through his notes. "You said you were jumped when taking the garbage out. Is that correct?"

"Yes."

He looked down at his notes. "They held a knife to your face, walked you to the open back door, and ordered you to go to the office and pull the power on the cameras." He looked up. "Correct?"

"Yeah. I told you that already."

"You didn't add that they stopped on the back step before entering the store and examined the ceiling. Nor did you tell us if they asked about a camera system or where the cameras fed to. A lot of stores have cameras that feed online. Store owners can watch the footage from the comfort of their own homes. If these thugs were aware of double-checking the camera in the back room, how did they know there was only one back there? And how did they know you actually cut the power to the feed and didn't leave it running before they entered the back door?"

Marcus shrugged. "I'm not a criminal. I have no idea what they think."

The tall cop stared at him for a long moment. "You're aware we're going to watch the store's cameras, correct?"

Marcus nodded, his stomach turning and twisting. What if they suspected him even though his story was perfect? He wondered how many people in his position would cut themselves as badly as he did just to hide their own crime.

"You're also aware that we have to talk to other employees and past employees, right?"

"What's that got to do with me?" he asked. "However you do your job is up to you. I was doing my job tonight when I was jumped. I hope you talk to everybody and try to find the assholes that did this."

Both cops slipped their notebooks away.

"We'll make some calls and wait until you're stitched up. Then we want to come back and talk to you about something else."

"What else could there be to talk about? When the doctors are done here, I'm going home. I'm tired. It's been a long night."

"Let's just say." The tall, angrier man looked at his partner, who nodded. He turned back to look at Marcus. "Let's just say we don't believe a word of your statement."

Marcus broke out in a cold sweat. He hoped his face hadn't paled too much.

"We do this for a living. We've heard every story and every way crimes are committed. Something isn't right about what you said tonight. And it's all leading to one conclusion."

Marcus was afraid to speak but had to ask. He only hoped his voice wouldn't betray him.

"What conclusion?"

The curtain pulled back, and a doctor stepped in past the officers.

"Let me get a look at that," the doctor said. He gestured at the officers. "Am I interrupting something here?"

"No, we were just leaving. When you're done, Marcus, we will talk again."

Both cops disappeared behind the curtain, and the doctor got to work on the stitches.

Marcus wasn't sure what hurt more. The needle cleaving his flesh when he was stitched up, or the fact that the cops saw through his entire plan.

Chapter 4

THE DOCTOR FINISHED QUICKLY and left after putting a new bandage over the stitches. It gave Marcus time to think about what his approach to the police would be. He had hope. He still believed he could walk away from this as long as he stuck to his story.

The police worked on evidence and proof. Nothing motivated them more than absolute proof. If they didn't get proof, they couldn't convict, which meant they wouldn't even charge him unless it was to scare him into confessing.

Maybe that was their angle. Maybe they wanted him to give himself up.

He would never speak the truth. He would always say that two guys jumped him wearing masks. He got knifed in the face, and they broke the safe and stole the money. Of course, he told the robbers about the camera. He had a knife against his cheek.

That's what he would recite in his sleep. That was the story he would stick to until his dying day.

Fuck them if they thought it was him.

Footsteps approached from the other side of the curtain.

He readied himself for the battle of wits he was about to have.

To start, he would get them off balance by asking their names. Maybe he would ask for their badge numbers if they questioned him too hard. He knew that was his right. He could even say he wanted a lawyer and wouldn't speak another word without one.

As long as he didn't waver from his story, nothing could happen to him, and he could keep the money.

The curtain billowed as the footsteps stopped near the edge. Whoever was there just stood and waited against the edge of the curtain.

"Hello?" Marcus said.

Maybe it had been his imagination.

"Doctor?"

A hand curled around the opening in the curtain, and a man entered.

"Who are you?" Marcus asked.

The medium-built man wore jeans and a black hoodie with the hood up, covering his head and most of his face. Marcus owned a black one just like it. Only the edge of the man's nose was exposed.

"Tell them," the man said in a deep, oddly familiar voice, "that your boss Frankie did this."

"What? Who are you?"

"That is not important," Deep Voice said. "Tell them you think it was Frankie."

Marcus crossed his arms on his chest. "I know what happened. I'll tell them the truth as I know it. Let me see your face."

The visitor ignored Marcus. "Katy's life depends on this. Don't be a stubborn fool."

Marcus tried to get up on one elbow at the mention of Katy's name.

"How dare you—who are you?"

The man moved fast, pushing on Marcus's shoulder and shoving him back into the bed.

"You're not a hero," the visitor whispered between clenched teeth. "Don't try to be a tough guy. Just tell them it had to do with Frankie. You're sure of it. The two guys had to have been sent from Frankie. Maybe add that you thought they said his name or something."

"Why would Frankie rob his own store? And how does Katy come into this?" Marcus asked. "And who the fuck are you to know all that?"

The man's face had become partially exposed this close. Marcus recognized his lips, nose, and the timbre of the man's voice. This was someone he knew and knew well, but he couldn't put a name to the face. Maybe if he saw the man's eyes.

"Don't worry about why Frankie would do this or that." The man moved toward the opening in the curtain. "Katy comes into this because of you. She could be in trouble if you don't do what I've asked."

"I'm confused. You're not making sense. How could she be in trouble when I was the one who was robbed? The guys got away." He had to give everyone the same story. "No one involved in this even knows who Katy is."

The man pulled his off hoodie. He stood with only the left side of his face toward Marcus, but Marcus saw enough to know why he recognized the features and the voice.

Marcus pushed back into the pillow so hard it rose around his ears, then squished flat.

"Who …?" Marcus tried to ask, but his throat caught and closed. He swallowed and tried again. "Who are you?"

The man had an uncanny resemblance to Marcus himself. They were so close in appearance. They could be brothers.

Twin brothers. A doppelgänger. Just like his father said on the phone.

"Tell them what I told you. Save Katy." The man turned and faced him directly. "For us."

On the man's right cheek, a bandage was pasted at the exact same place as Marcus's knife wound.

It was like staring into a mirror.

Am I losing my mind?

The man's attention appeared to be on something besides Marcus. Then he looked at something else. Marcus followed his gaze but couldn't determine what had drawn his body double to look that way.

"I have to go," the visitor said, seemingly distracted by something like a cat watching phantoms move about the room.

"Wait," Marcus said. "What did you mean when you said, 'save Katy for us'?"

Footsteps approached from the other side of the curtain.

The cops were returning.

The man jerked toward the curtain, grabbed his hoodie, and flipped it over his head. Then he pulled the curtain back, slipped out, and disappeared.

As the curtain folded back in place, it was immediately ripped open, and the two officers stepped inside the cubicle.

"Who were you talking to?" the tall cop asked.

"You didn't see him?"

"I wouldn't ask if I had."

"He stepped out as you came in. The curtain was still moving when you touched it."

The officers exchanged a glance.

Marcus lowered himself back onto the bed and got into a more comfortable position. He had to bring himself around to reality. There was no possible explanation for what had just happened. He had to assume it didn't happen.

Or was that what his father had to talk to him about? That he had a twin brother all this time, and no one told him?

But with a bandage in the exact same spot?

Highly unlikely.

What should he tell the cops now? His made-up story, or blame Frankie as his doppelgänger told him to?

The phone call from his father echoed throughout his head.

I have to tell you the truth, his father had said. *Have you ever seen yourself?*

What did his father know? What could he know? Ever since Marcus's mother died twenty years ago, he had been trying to drink himself into an early grave. Marcus was surprised the old man was still alive.

The officers pulled their notebooks out again.

"Is there anything else you want to add to your version of the events?" the taller one asked.

Marcus thought about it for a moment. Should he stick to the story or go with what the strange visitor asked of him?

Have you ever seen yourself?

Save Katy. For us.

Now that he had *seen himself* and his father knew some kind of *truth*, maybe there was something to the visitor's story. Could Katy be in trouble? Had a ripple effect started because of what happened at the store?

He made up his mind at that moment. "Yes, I want to add who might have hired the two guys who robbed the store."

Both cops raised their eyebrows.

"But first," Marcus said. "I'd like to know who I'm speaking with. You both know me, but neither of you introduced yourselves."

The men pulled out ID, flashed it, then dropped business cards on the side table.

"I'm Detective Bruce Green," the tall one said. "This is Detective

Jacob Smith."

"Thank you." Marcus picked up their cards and examined them. Before looking up, he said, "I would like to add something to my statement."

Detective Green readied his pen and waited.

"I think my boss had something to do with it."

Green frowned. "How's that?"

"I'm not sure, but I thought I heard the two guys who jumped me say Frankie's name at one point."

"Just because they said his name doesn't mean he's behind it. Maybe the robbers simply knew the owner. Why didn't you say this before?"

"Because I didn't want to get Frankie in trouble."

Detective Smith put his pad away without writing anything down. Detective Green did, too.

"That's what we thought," Green said.

"Really?" Marcus sat up straighter. "Seriously? You guys thought Frankie was involved?"

"Are you aware of Frankie's business dealings?"

Marcus gave a short shake of his head. "Not really, no." A thought occurred to him. "That would explain how the guys who jumped me knew where the camera system was. Wow, it's all making sense." Marcus shook his head. "Frankie's in Los Angeles at a trade show right now."

Detective Green waved a finger back and forth. "No, he's not."

"What?"

"Frankie didn't leave Toronto this weekend. He's in jail."

Marcus's heart raced to catch up to his breathing. "What the hell are you talking about?"

"He serves his time on weekends. This was his last weekend."

That explained a lot. Frankie was never around on the weekends.

Marcus always did the Saturdays and Sundays. Frankie had pumped Marcus up a year ago, saying that his sales were so good he needed him to manage the weekends for a while, and he gave him his only raise to do just that.

"What's he in for?" Marcus asked.

"You should ask him yourself."

Marcus felt betrayed by Frankie. They had been close. Sure Marcus had built the store up for Frankie, and he hadn't been rewarded financially, but Frankie had treated him well. And all this time, Frankie had been lying to him. Now the tables had turned. Hadn't *he* just betrayed Frankie?

"You find something funny?" Detective Smith asked.

Marcus stopped smiling. "Just that Frankie's been lying to me all this time, and I had no idea. Now someone robbed his store for him. Just thought it was kind of poetic."

"Poetic, huh?" Green said. "Why would Frankie hold up his own store?"

"No idea. Isn't that your job?"

"You want us to do our job?" Green asked. He stepped around the bed and walked up to Marcus's side. "Okay, here's me doing my job. We don't think there were two guys who jumped you and robbed the store tonight."

Keep a stone face, he told himself. *Don't even blink.*

"We think you did this all on your own and made the whole story up about being robbed. So why not just tell us the truth, and we'll go easy on you."

"You want the truth?" Marcus asked, clenching his teeth. He thought about Katy. He thought about what his body double said. And he decided to stay on course.

"The truth is what I already told you it is. Now leave me alone. Go do your jobs like good little cops, or the next question I ask is your badge numbers. I'm gonna want them for my lawyer when we beat this case because two idiot detectives tried to scare and intimidate the wounded store clerk while he was still in the hospital."

He had no idea where that came from, but it was empowering to be so strong.

"What's this all about?" Katy asked as she pulled the curtain back and stepped in. "Is everything okay, Marcus?"

"These two fine detectives were just leaving."

Green nodded at Smith. They walked to the curtain, stepped around Katy, and stopped at the edge of the cubicle.

"You've got our cards," Detective Green said. "Call us if you think of anything else, anything at all. And don't worry, we'll do our jobs. But if we find out you've been lying to us, we'll come for you, and it won't be to just chat. I'm sure you understand." He let the curtain fall, then added, "Stay in Toronto. Make sure we can find you when we need to."

Their footsteps echoed in the quiet hospital at this early hour.

Marcus reached for Katy's hand.

"What was that all about?" Katy asked.

"Frankie's in jail."

"What?" Her eyes widened, and she turned to face him.

"He's been lying to us this whole time. It looks like the two guys that robbed the place tonight were sent by Frankie. The police are working on a theory and just wanted to make sure I told them everything."

"They sure have an aggressive way of covering all the bases." She sidled up next to him on the bed. "Something weird happened after I got my coffee."

"What?"

"I was walking back here and thought you called my name in the hallway. I was sure it was you, but when I looked back, the corridor was empty."

"That is weird. It couldn't have happened. I've been here the whole time."

She shook her head. "You're right. Weird." She rubbed his arm. "Can I take you home now?"

"Please. Get me out of here. Where's your car?"

"We'll take a taxi back to the store to pick it up. I'll drive us home from there."

Meandering through the hospital corridors, he couldn't shake the feeling of being watched by another Marcus Johnson.

If he had an identical twin, why did his dad keep it from him all these years?

An image of the bandage on the man's face popped into his head. If Marcus had a twin, why did the twin brother have the same cut on his face in the same spot, sporting an identical bandage?

Chapter 5

Sleep remained elusive. Soft light broke through the sheer curtains in their bedroom as the sun rose on another Monday morning in July.

With his adrenaline low, the pain in his face pulsed with his heartbeat. He didn't want to move a muscle, especially not a facial muscle.

The thought of hiccups or a cough made him shudder. He wondered what possessed him to dig as deep as he did into his cheek with the knife. So deep that stitches were required. He could have caused nerve damage. What had he been thinking?

But he knew what he was thinking.

Authenticity.

It had to look like someone else cut him. If he stole the money and wanted to get away with it, a paper cut wouldn't work.

The knife.

Looking back over the last twelve hours, examining and reexamining the entire episode, he couldn't see anything wrong with what he did.

Except for the knife.

Not that there was anything wrong with the knife. He knew where it was. His fingerprints were still on it because he had removed the gloves and tossed them in his car. Then he had used the knife to cut himself.

All he had to do was get the knife when he went back for his car later in the day.

Leaving his car, there was part of the plan. Racing back to retrieve it after leaving the hospital might have seemed out of the ordinary since Katy's car was there, and she could drive him home.

They had left the hospital after four in the morning and decided to go home, get some rest, and then head over in the afternoon to pick up his car.

No one would search his car without a warrant, and the detectives wouldn't get a judge to sign a warrant to search his car in the first twenty-four hours without a lot more to go on.

He had to continue to act as normal as possible. All decisions and actions needed to come from the place that *he* was robbed.

But what about Frankie?

What the hell was up with all the lying? Jail? On the weekends?

He'd known Frankie for two years. He had an Italian heritage but treated Marcus like a brother, a member of his family. Frankie had told him secrets he was sure even his closest confidantes didn't know.

Sure, Frankie had a tough go of it on the streets of Toronto in his early days, but he was clean now. A real businessman. As far as Marcus knew, all his past associates were exactly that, past associates.

He looked at Katy's face. The blankets covered her up to her neck. She looked so comfortable in her slumber, her breathing deep and rhythmic.

Slowly, he lifted the sheets and eased off the bed, trying not to move the bed too much.

Without getting dressed, he used the minute amount of light filtering through the curtains to make his way out of the bedroom, down the hall, and into the bathroom.

He closed the door without a sound and started the bathtub. A hot bath would soothe his muscles and ease the tension. He needed to relax, let it all go, and then try to sleep again.

This morning's shift was his at the store, but that wasn't going to happen. Maybe he would get Katy to drive him over in the afternoon, and he would work for a few hours to clean up the back of the store.

She might not like that idea, but he needed to get that knife and make it disappear. He needed to get his car to retrieve the cash and stash it somewhere safer than under the driver's seat in a tennis ball container.

The tub was almost full. He turned the water off and climbed in, one foot at a time. When he flicked off the bathroom's light switch, it activated the red nightlight. That was all the light he needed.

He sank slowly into the hot water. After his body had acclimated to the temperature, he lay back, resting his arms and hands on the sides of the tub.

He had closed his eyes and was breathing in the moist air from the hot water when he thought he heard a noise.

He sat up slowly, so he didn't slosh the water too much and listened, his head cocked sideways.

Would his doppelgänger show up and walk right into the house? Did someone knock on the front door?

The knob of the bathroom door turned.

He started, and some water splashed over the tub's edge.

"What …"

Katy stepped in. "I thought you were in here. I wasn't so sure when I didn't see the light under the door." She smiled in the red glow of the nightlight. "What's going on?"

"Couldn't sleep," he said and settled back in the tub.

"Makes sense. What you've been through would keep anyone up

all night." She closed the door to keep the warmer air in.

"What have I been through?" he asked.

She frowned and sat on the toilet lid beside the tub. He lay back in his resting position and stretched out.

"You don't remember what happened only hours ago?" she asked with a sly smile.

A crazy thought that the Alzheimer's mutant gene had already started working on him struck him hard. He hated when someone asked him about his memory. But he never told Katy that because he didn't want her to treat him any differently.

"Of course, I remember."

"Not only was it a scary ordeal at the store, but you also found out your boss is in jail." She placed a hand on his. "What if this is somehow connected? What if Frankie's past caught up with him, and you paid the price for it?"

Marcus shook his head and looked down at the water. "I don't think so. If that is what happened, and I find out this—" he pointed at the bandage on his face— "was because of Frankie, I'll be pretty pissed."

"What would you do? Get another job?"

"I'm not skilled in anything."

"You have half a dozen years in retail. Maybe you could apply to be a manager or something. Step it up a bit."

"Maybe I should've stayed in school or opened my own business so none of this would be happening."

"We both know why you dropped out."

"Yeah, I let my Alzheimer's win. Since I was going to get it in my thirties or forties, I wanted to live my life to the fullest and have fun. So I quit school, partied, and had too much fun. By the time I was in my mid-twenties, all my friends were off with their careers and getting married."

"We all make decisions at certain times in our lives that are valid then. Some come back to haunt us, others don't. But you don't have to allow the past to dictate the future. You could change things now." Katy pointed at the plaque on the wall. "Remember when you gave me that?"

There was the word remember again.

He nodded, not wanting to open his mouth and say something he'd regret because she had used the word 'remember' twice.

"I love its message. 'It all started because two people fell in love.'" She looked at him in that cute way he loved, a half-smile on her face. "That's us. If you hadn't chosen this path, we wouldn't have met. You would've been working somewhere else, building your career."

"What now?" he asked.

"What do you mean, 'what now'? You can do anything you want."

He lowered himself into the water until it wrapped around the base of his neck.

"How? Go to school? By the time I finish, I'll be losing my memory. That gets in the way of a career."

Katy looked at her hands and fidgeted with a nail.

"Look," Marcus said. "I'm sorry."

"It's okay."

"I've been through a lot tonight, and I'm just trying to process everything. I haven't been this disoriented in a long time. Not since I was a kid."

"I understand."

"I appreciate your attempts to help. Maybe when this is all over, we can revisit the idea about going back to school and looking for a better job."

She nodded and looked up at him with a smile, the kind that was meant only for him.

"Later today, could you drive me to the store?" Marcus asked.

"You plan on going back today?"

"Yeah. I gotta go clean up a bit. Maybe I'll open for a few hours. It's my regularly scheduled shift."

"You're not worried?"

"What, that the bad guys will return?" He shook his head, the water rippling from the movement. "Not in the least. Why would they? The safe is empty, and the store hasn't made any money since they robbed it."

"When's Frankie due back?"

"Last I heard from him, tomorrow."

"Do you think this is connected to him?"

"No idea. Probably not, but it makes sense the police have his name pop up since he owns the store and he's spending time in jail on the weekends."

"Okay," Katy said. "I'll put on some tea and meet you in the living room when you're done."

"Thanks, Honey."

She got off the toilet and leaned down to kiss his forehead.

"Katy?" Marcus asked.

"Yeah?" She stopped with her hand on the door handle.

"After work, I'm going to drive up to my dad's place."

She let go of the handle and leaned against the sink. "Really? Why today?"

"He called last night." Marcus met her eyes. "Before the robbery. I heard something outside by the back door when I was on the phone with him."

"Wow, really? That's important. Did you tell the detectives?"

"No, I forgot."

"Was what you heard loud enough for your dad to hear it?"

"Even if it was, he couldn't hear a thing. He could barely hear me."

"Drunk?"

Marcus nodded.

"I'm sorry."

"It's okay. That's his story. That's who he is now. After Mom died, he was good to me for a few years. I had to leave when I was fifteen. He's been utterly drunk ever since."

"Doesn't make it any easier, though."

"I know. But he said something strange last night."

"What?"

Marcus inhaled deeply, wondering how much to tell her. The old Marcus told Katy everything. No secrets. This new one had to start qualifying things. That scared him. "He asked if I'd seen myself lately."

"Seen yourself?"

"Yeah, I know. Crazy, huh?"

"As you said, drunk."

"I should still go by and see him. I haven't been there since Christmas."

"And for a good reason."

"Anyway, just thought I'd let you know I'll be later getting home tonight."

She stepped into the hallway and patted her pant leg. "I've got gauze and extra bandages in my pocket here. Maybe we'll change that bandage when you come down for tea—"

The doorbell rang.

They both jumped.

Marcus got his feet under him and stood up to towel off. "Who the hell could that be at this hour? Damn, it's probably only seven or eight in the morning."

"The police?" Katy guessed as she opened the bathroom door.

"Katy, wait. Let me answer it." The doorbell rang again. Then once more. "Determined, aren't they?"

Katy waited until Marcus got out. He walked past her and down the hall to their bedroom. As he sat on the bed to slip into his jeans, the early morning visitor banged on the door four times with what sounded like a hammer.

"I'm coming!" Marcus yelled. Then under his breath, "For fuck sake."

He grabbed a T-shirt from the chair in the corner where he piled his clothes. On the way over his head, the T-shirt caught the lip of the bandage and tugged on it slightly. He gasped at the sharp pain.

"You okay?" Katy asked.

"Yeah."

He headed for the door, pain fueling his anger as the visitor knocked again, harder and faster.

"Coming!" Marcus yelled.

He grabbed the doorknob and yanked it open.

Two men stood on his porch. Both had barrel chests and matching hairstyles, long and pulled back in a ponytail. The one on the right had graying hair and a gray goatee. The leather they wore was solid black.

"Looks like you two bikers got the wrong address. Do you know what time it is?"

"Marcus Johnson?" the one with gray hair asked.

When he spoke, Marcus saw a batch of missing teeth. These men looked and breathed fighting. Something about them made him think of caged animals, all the pent-up venom oozing from their aura.

"Who's asking?"

"Mohammed," the man raised a fist and gestured to it as if Mohammed was the name of his fist. "Ali," he added, gesturing to his other fist. "Come with us without trouble, or you get to meet the boxing great, live, right here on your doorstep. So, what'll it be?"

The pit of Marcus's stomach had that Duracell battery rotting in it again. Thoughts of who these men were and why they were sent raced through his mind, but he couldn't come up with anything that made sense.

"You going to give me anything else? Like who you are and where we're supposed to be going?"

"Frankie sent us," the younger biker said. "He wants to talk."

"The telephone would've worked great. Thanks, but no thanks. Tell him I'll call. In fact, tell him I'm at the store later this after—"

The hand came fast. Marcus didn't have time to blink. Open palmed, it slapped him on the cheek with the stitches. Red-hot pain flared so fast and intense that he felt instantly dizzy, and the world wavered in his vision. He grabbed for the doorframe to steady himself.

Katy screamed his name from behind him.

Rough hands gripped both his arms and yanked him off the porch. Then he was airborne. He landed hard on the grass of his front lawn.

He rolled over and looked up, trying to catch his breath, a hand protectively covering his wounded cheek.

"What the fuck, man?" he gasped without moving his mouth too much. "What the hell was that for?"

"I warned you. Come with us. No trouble. But no, you wanted trouble, so that's what you get."

"Okay, okay, take it easy. I'll go with you."

As he rolled onto his stomach and got his knees under him, he looked back at the front door. Katy had both hands by her mouth, which was as wide in surprise as her eyes were. He tried to wink at her in reassurance, but all he ended up doing was blinking.

"It's okay, baby. I'll be home soon. It's Frankie. He's probably pissed about the store. Don't worry. You know how he gets."

The one with the gray goatee stuck a hand under Marcus's arm and lifted him to his feet. They stood like that, five feet from the front door, as Katy started to close the door, no doubt to call the police.

The detectives' cards were still in the pants he wore last night. Hopefully, she would call the same detectives who worked the robbery last night. They would love to know Frankie orchestrated Marcus's kidnapping at eight in the morning.

The younger biker was still on the porch. His foot shot out and stopped the door from closing.

"What are you doing?" Marcus asked him.

"I think I'll keep the missus company until you return."

Fear and anger collided. A well of pressure roiled through him. "The fuck you will. Step off that porch, or I'll break your leg."

Marcus realized at that moment how useless a threat like that was to a man like the one standing on his porch. This was the bikers' tennis match. Their court. Their racket and balls. Marcus was just a guest and would lose any game he tried to play against men like these. He was nothing like them. But that made him hate them even more. The power they wielded just because they'd lived a tougher life.

Deep down inside, an animal instinct roared from a stillness long asleep. He allowed its release. Felt survival in its presence. Felt power in its rise. A fire roared in his veins as the pain in his face waned.

"You want to repeat yourself, tough guy?" the biker on the porch asked.

The gray-haired biker beside him let go of his arm. Marcus knew it was so he could pull the hand back and take another shot at him.

But that wasn't going to happen.

Tough guys or not, they still felt pain, just like everyone else. They still bled like any other man.

He dropped his head fast to avoid the fist coming his way, then raised his foot and brought it down hard on the side of the biker's knee, driving him to the ground.

The gray-haired biker grunted under pressure. A second later, he was on his knees in front of Marcus.

Still standing on the back of the man's leg, Marcus shifted his weight and used his other leg to kick at the biker's face.

Something cracked audibly when he connected. Blood squirted in a fountain from the center of the biker's face. The man's nose was smashed almost completely sideways.

The biker with fists named after the famous boxer fell to the grass in slow motion, both hands covering his nose in an attempt to staunch the blood flow.

"Katy, shut and lock the door," Marcus yelled.

He stepped off the biker's leg and jumped away, heading for the back of the house, away from the biker on the porch.

"Call the police!" he yelled over his shoulder.

The younger biker jumped over his partner and gave chase, pulling a black gun from inside his jacket.

Would he really shoot me? In the back?

Marcus ran as if his life depended on it. At the corner of the house, he looked back one more time.

The gun was aimed at him.

Holy shit!

Marcus turned the corner of the house in his bare feet and disappeared into thin air.

Chapter 6

THE MAN UNDER MARCUS'S foot rolled to the ground with blood seeping from his nose. As his partner pulled his foot from the edge of the door to approach Marcus, Katy seized her opportunity, slammed the front door shut, and locked it.

Marcus had yelled something, but she was already running to the back of the house, heading for the kitchen phone. Her legs threatened to give out, but she pushed on, only bumping into the hallway wall once.

Her breathing ragged, and she gulped air as she grabbed the phone. Her sweaty palms fumbled and almost dropped it, then squeezed tighter to maintain control as she hit 911.

She brought it to her ear.

A dial tone.

"Shit."

She had dialed so fast it hadn't gone through.

Something hard hit the door to her right. She hoped it was Marcus so she could let him in, but it wasn't.

The younger biker's face was pushed up against the glass. He was smiling, a black gun in his hand aimed at her from four feet away.

Blackness clouded the edges of her vision. She grabbed the countertop for balance, almost dropping the phone again.

"Open the door, or I'll shoot through the glass," the biker shouted.

He tapped the glass with the tip of the gun.

Katy set the phone down. Dazed, she unlocked the back door.

The biker's body checked her, knocking her to the floor where her robe flipped open to the waist.

His face lit up as she frantically tried to cover herself. Her stomach clenched. She wondered if she would look so desirable with vomit all over her chest. Then she decided she didn't want to know.

"What do—" her throat caught. "What do you want?"

"Where's Marcus?" the biker asked. He locked the back door behind him.

She was surprised she could think so clearly. "Why are you asking me? You were the one chasing him."

The biker stepped forward and kicked her leg.

She grunted and drew her legs up close until she could wrap her arms around them. Against her will, she started to cry.

"Your backyard is big," the man said. "There's no fence."

"So?"

"That means the only place he could've gone was back inside the house."

"How? Through the door that I had to unlock for you? And you think if he came through that door, I would take the time to re-lock it and stand by the phone knowing you were right behind him?"

"I don't know what you're talking about, bitch. All I know is I was only five or six feet behind him when he turned the corner. After I turned the corner, he was gone. Disappeared."

"Disappeared …" Katy repeated, wondering what that meant and where Marcus could've gone.

"Get up," the man ordered.

"Why?"

His face reddened as he bent over. "Because I said so," he hissed.

Katy got to her feet slowly, her legs shaky.

"I'm taking her with me," the biker shouted down the hallway.

"Marcus isn't in the house," Katy said.

"Whatever you say, bitch."

He grabbed her arm in a vise grip, half pulled, half dragged her down the hall toward the front of the house. He had slipped the gun away, freeing up his other hand.

At the front door, he unlocked and opened it. His partner had picked himself up and walked to a black van parked by the curb.

"Last chance, asshole," the biker shouted. "We're either taking you or your woman."

Katy struggled under the man's grip. Any second, Marcus would pop up and stop this madness.

Katy wondered why Frankie would send biker thugs to pick Marcus up. What was Frankie mixed up in?

"Let me go." Katy struggled under his grip. "Kidnapping is serious jail time."

"I'm not kidnapping you, you stupid bitch. You're coming willingly." He looked at his partner. "Ain't that right, John?"

John responded with an indiscernible grunt.

Something hit her in the head. The wall came fast, smacking her above the ear. The world spun as her eyes jerked in their sockets, then rose skyward.

She crumpled to the floor, her face bouncing once on the welcome mat.

Chapter 7

Marcus opened his eyes. He still wore his T-shirt, jeans, and nothing on his feet. His chest inflated and deflated rapidly from running around the side of the house in his effort to escape the insane biker with the gun.

But now he was standing in the parking lot of The Act of Love.

What the hell is going on? How did I get here?

The night was relatively warm, but a chill covered his flesh, goose bumps rose on his arms, and he shivered. He scanned the area and saw nothing out of the ordinary.

A random car drove by. The sidewalk was empty. It was late, just like last night.

He touched his face and ran his hands along the bandage's edges to ensure it was still affixed properly.

How did I get here? he asked himself again.

There was no rational explanation. Ever since he had robbed the store, nothing had made sense.

One minute ago, it was eight in the morning, and he was running through his backyard. Now he stood barefoot at the edge of the large parking lot in front of the store. At night.

He looked at Frankie's store. The place that set everything in motion.

Stars raced around the edge of his vision. He had to get his breathing under control, or he would pass out.

The only car in the entire area was his. It was parked in the exact spot where he had put it last night.

But he'd left it there, so, of course, it would still be there.

The lights in The Act of Love turned off.

His eyes widened. One foot in front of the other, he walked toward the base of the light standard in the parking lot to watch what would happen next.

At the front window of the store, someone walked up and locked the door. That person stopped at the window and stared out.

Marcus leaned against the post, mostly hiding behind it, and stared at the window to see who was inside.

A fuzzy glimmer of light passed by the front of the store. A car door slammed somewhere.

He glanced around but saw no one.

He rubbed his eyes and refocused on the front of the store.

The man in the store stared back at him.

No way. I refuse to believe it.

The man in the store was him, minus the bandage.

It hit him like a brick in the forehead.

Last night when he locked up and stared out the window, he had seen someone familiar staring back at him from the parking lot's light standard. That someone appeared to be crying and was dressed exactly as he was right now.

Fuzzy lights flashed by his vision again.

What the hell is that?

He looked away from the light standard. With one more glance over his shoulder at the front of the store, he ran to the sidewalk and started along it as more crazy lights passed by his vision.

"What's happening?" he yelled out loud.

Even though he was in an industrial area, the subtle silhouette of houses formed to his left and right out of nothing. One second they weren't there, the next, they were. He could see through the images of the houses to the strip mall across the street that was closed up for the night.

The houses wavered and glowed green like the northern lights had landed and surrounded him. The lights formed shapes he would see in any residential area.

At that moment, he was convinced his Early Onset Alzheimer's disease had set in. There could be nothing else to explain this craziness.

A whooping sound coupled with a high-pitched screech accompanied the lights of the residential street as they brightened.

A bump, like the nudge of an elevator stopping on a floor, shook him.

The nighttime street of the industrial area completely disappeared.

The sun shone through clouds high in the sky. His feet cooled in the morning grass of the backyard of his house.

He was back.

But his mind wasn't.

It shut down. His internal lights dimmed as he fainted and fell to the lawn.

Chapter 8

Marcus opened his eyes.

He was still behind his house. The sun hadn't moved much. He must've only been out for a few minutes.

He got to his feet and looked around to see if anyone was watching.

It had to be a dream. All of it was a crazy dream.

He couldn't sleep last night and had a bath, talked to Katy, and then came outside and passed out on the grass.

But I was at the store and saw myself.

A dream.

He adjusted his pants and fixed his T-shirt. All he needed was a hot shower and a hotter coffee.

He tried the back door, but it was locked.

He knocked, but after three tries, Katy didn't come.

Maybe she's still asleep.

He jumped off the back deck and started around to the front of the house, fearing what he would find there. Had this really been a dream? If it wasn't, then what actually happened? How could he have gone back in time to last night?

The bikers showing up, giving chase, and then him waking up on the grass all made sense. But being in front of the store last night didn't add up. And those moving lights and shimmering houses … what the hell was that?

But if it were true, he had to have lost his mind. In the real world, where laws of gravity and physics are absolute, what happened was impossible. The images in his mind were restricted to a playground in an asylum. It had no basis in reality—yet it felt as real as this very moment.

And what about the man who looked exactly like him in the hospital earlier? Could that have been him, traveling there from some other dimension in time?

He clapped his hands together loudly in an attempt to banish the crazy thoughts.

At the front of the house, the biker's black van was gone.

Yeah, because it had never been there in the first place. I simply passed out in my yard in the middle of the night.

He walked up the front steps and stopped.

The door sat wide open.

In a tentative voice, he said, "Katy?"

Not trusting what he would find, he looked at the grass where he had tussled with the gray-haired biker. A blemish colored the grass from the biker's bleeding nose. From where he stood, it looked black, but it could've easily been dark red.

The dark red of blood from a broken nose.

Blood spread in a splat formation on the doorframe. The welcome mat had more blood, pooled in a small puddle, drying at the edges.

Someone had hit the frame hard enough to shoot blood across the trim and then dropped to the welcome mat, where they bled enough to cause the puddle.

Bloody drips led away from the puddle, down the steps, and were lost to the grass.

What the hell happened here?

"Katy?" he called louder.

He ran into the house, screaming Katy's name as police sirens wailed in the distance.

He had a feeling they were coming to his home.

After scouring the first floor, he ran upstairs. Maybe Katy was in their bedroom, still asleep.

At the bedroom door, when she was nowhere in sight, he came to the conclusion he'd been trying to avoid.

The blood on the doorframe and the welcome mat was Katy's. The bikers were real. The reason their van was gone was because they hurt her and then took her with them in his place.

He struggled to avoid thinking about what they could possibly be doing with her.

He turned around as if in a dream and walked the length of the hallway until he stood outside the bathroom door.

The bathtub was still full.

His eyes blurred as he looked at the toilet seat Katy had sat on when they talked. He wiped the tears from both eyes as he looked above the toilet to the plaque he had bought Katy when they moved in together.

It all started because two people fell in love, and it would end because two people were in love.

The police sirens stopped outside the house with a screech of tires.

Marcus walked down the stairs, through the foyer, and out the front door.

Two police cruisers and one unmarked sedan parked where the biker's van had parked.

Three uniformed officers jumped out of the cruisers.

The two men who stepped out of the unmarked car were the

detectives from the hospital, Smith, and Green.

"Hey, guys, what's up?" Marcus said as they approached him on the front steps, doing everything he could to look and act calm.

Green spoke first. "We got a domestic dispute call at this address. Everything okay, Johnson?"

"No one here but little old me."

There was no way to explain his sudden departure, and even though Katy wasn't here, he refused to believe Frankie would have her harmed. That meant no cops.

Green closed the distance between them and stood at the base of the front steps. Marcus moved off the front porch so they would talk on the grass. He didn't want either detective seeing the blood on the welcome mat.

"Two different people," Green said, "your neighbors called 911. Are you saying they were both wrong?"

Detective Smith had moved back and talked to the uniformed men, who then spread out and walked in pairs around either side of the house.

"What are they doing?" Marcus asked.

"Securing the perimeter."

"What perimeter? My house is secure."

"Marcus Johnson," Detective Green said.

"What?" He glared at the detective. This wasn't the first time he wondered where the well of hostility rose from.

"Didn't get much sleep?" the detective asked.

"Look, whatever those 911 callers saw, I can't speak for, but everything is fine now."

"Fine, now? Wasn't it fine before? You're implying something was wrong earlier if it is fine now."

"You know what I mean." Marcus's stomach twisted.

Green stepped in, crowding him, forcing Marcus to move back.

"Marcus?" Green said.

"What?"

"There was a robbery at the store you worked at last night."

"I know. I was there."

"Let me finish."

Two officers came into view after walking around the house. Both men shook their heads.

"After the robbery, you come home, and we get a call about an altercation on your front lawn this morning. A domestic dispute is scary for my officers because, as a cop, you just never know what you're walking into when a domestic call comes in. And since I have anything with your name and address flagged as my partner and I are working your robbery—"

"It wasn't *my* robbery!" Marcus snapped.

"You know what I mean. When we saw the address, we had to respond."

"Okay, fine. Now you can go. Everything's fine here."

"You've changed since last night. You weren't like this when you gave us your statement."

"I'm cranky. I'm tired. I was held up last night, and I couldn't sleep. Now I have neighbors calling the cops on me, and I have you on my front lawn. That's a lot to handle in twelve hours. Life was pretty quiet before this. Now it's time to go back to the quiet life."

Green raised his hands and stepped back. "Fair enough. If you say nothing's going on, I believe you. But I have one more question."

"Of course you do."

"When you heard the sirens a minute ago, why open your front door and step out to meet us? Why assume they were for you and not for a car accident a block away or something else if nothing was happening here?"

"I saw you pull up from the window."

"Bullshit. I looked. You weren't in the window."

Marcus glared at him. He felt violated to be always called on everything he said, and it was obvious Detective Green didn't believe a word of his story.

"I'm going back inside my house, and I'm going to sleep. So if we're done here, I'll be on my way, as should you."

"Who is in the house with you?" Green asked.

"No one." Finally, something he could say with certainty.

Green walked around him and started for the front door. "Mind if we have a walk-through, take a look ourselves?"

"Wait." Marcus spun around and grabbed Green's arm.

Green stopped and looked down at his arm, where Marcus still held the inside of his elbow. Then Green raised his head and met Marcus's eyes.

Marcus let go of the man's arm. The other officer and Detective Smith came from the back corner of the house.

"Detective Smith?" Green called.

"Yeah?" Smith called back.

"How long would it take to get a warrant to search Marcus's house?"

"An hour. Maybe. Why?" Smith moved in close while the uniformed cops gathered by the road.

"It seems there's something in Marcus's house he doesn't want us to know about, and since he was involved in a suspicious robbery last night and now we have two different calls about a domestic on his front lawn, I'd say we have probable cause to just walk right in. Agree or disagree?"

"I'd agree," Smith said. He turned to the uniforms. "What about you guys? You okay with probable cause?"

All three men grunted in the affirmative.

There was nothing in the house that meant anything to Marcus.

The money from the robbery was still hidden in his car. The knife was still in the bushes behind the store. He just didn't want them seeing the blood on the welcome mat. He had no explanation for it, and telling them the truth would only get Frankie in more trouble. Sure he wanted Katy back, but harassing bikers and whoever Frankie was involved with wouldn't work using cops.

He had to talk to Frankie on his own, find out what was happening and fix whatever mistake he had made.

"So, how about it?" Green said. "You gonna give us permission to check the house out?"

"Get off my lawn," Marcus said. "Start walking back to your cruisers and leave." He breathed in deeply and clenched his fists. "I know my rights. Leave now."

Green raised his hands and stepped back at least four feet. "Whoa," he muttered. "Take it easy, tough guy. We're just trying to help. We're on your side."

Green continued to edge closer to the front door.

"What are you doing?" Marcus asked. "Your car is that way." The panic from an hour ago crept up on him. He pointed toward the road. "Go that way."

Green shouted toward the house. "Hey, Katy, you okay in there?"

Marcus started toward him.

Detective Green barked, "Watch yourself, Marcus. Threatening a peace officer is a serious offense."

Marcus stopped with a few feet between them. If Green turned around now, he would easily see the oval puddle of dark red blood by the welcome mat.

"You're acting aggressive," Green said. "Don't make me pepper spray you. My partner prefers the Taser. Step closer, and you can take a gamble on which of us hits you first."

Marcus didn't have a play. He couldn't move, and he knew it. He breathed through his mouth, trying to remain calm, waiting to see what Green was up to. He clenched and unclenched his hands, wishing these men would just get back in their cars and drive away.

"Katy?" Green shouted over his shoulder.

A door shut on the other side of the street. Marcus looked at the O'Conners, who lived directly across from him. Then another door opened at the Riley's house. The neighbors who called the police.

But what had they seen? What could they tell him about Katy? What would they tell the police?

Detective Green faced the house.

There was a moment of silence. Everything stood still for Marcus. The air ceased moving. The neighbors stopped walking. Even his heart stopped for a beat.

Then Detective Green slowly turned around, and the world spun on its axis again, sounds coming back to him. A bird chirped, and a car horn honked twice. A door opened, and an engine revved a block away.

"Detective Smith, please put Marcus in the cruiser. We're taking him downtown for a formal questioning where charges may be laid."

Marcus wanted to protest. He wanted to run. He wanted to find Katy and talk to Frankie. He wanted to do anything and everything but be dragged off his front lawn and placed into the back of a police cruiser for all his neighbors to see.

Arms grabbed him on either side, and he was led to the unmarked cruiser, where the doors locked from the outside.

Marcus knew Detective Green had seen the blood, and he understood what it was the moment he spotted it. The detective had credible calls to 911 regarding a domestic dispute, and it would be easy for an astute detective to figure out that Marcus wanted him out of his house. So he pushed the issue.

Then the detective saw the blood.

Of course, he would detain him.

But that wasn't the worst.

Katy was gone. She was with two angry bikers, and Marcus could only imagine what they were doing with her at that very moment.

He was sure the blood on the welcome mat was Katy's. If she were wounded and being tortured or raped because of what he did last night, he would never be able to live with that.

The pure horror of those thoughts was worse than anything the police would do to him.

By a long shot.

Chapter 9

"So you don't want to talk to us?" Detective Green asked.

Marcus stared down at the metal table his wrists were cuffed to.

They had gone through his house and searched it for over an hour while he waited in the back of the unmarked cruiser, lost in his own thoughts of terror for Katy.

When Detective Green came out, he had Marcus's black hoodie in his hands. He had tossed it in the back seat before they drove him downtown to the police station and placed him in this room.

Before cuffing him to the two chains that came up from the center of the table, Detective Green allowed him to slip into the hoodie to stave off shivers in the small, cold room.

Then they left him there for at least two more hours.

Both Smith and Green entered with the cliché coffee cup and didn't offer him one.

"There's nothing you want to say that'll add clarity to what's been happening since last night?" Green asked. After a few moments, Green spoke again. "Why not start with whose blood was on your doorstep?"

Yeah, sure. And I'll tell you all about how I escaped the bikers who were going to shoot me by time traveling.

The detectives looked at each other, then back at Marcus.

"We can do this all day," Green said. "Tonight, we'll go home, sleep in our warm beds and come back tomorrow for more silence if you want."

"You can only hold me for twenty-four hours without charging me."

"Wow, he talks." Green set his coffee down on the metal table. "That is true. But I'm sure we can charge you with something to keep you here for a while."

His stomach dropped. He needed out of here to go find Katy. He needed to talk to Frankie to find out why he sent bikers to his house.

He needed to get to his car. And he needed to destroy that knife so his prints wouldn't incriminate him.

"What's really going on, Marcus? Talk to us. We can help."

"No, you can't. No one can."

"Did you rob your own store last night?"

"I'm not saying another word. Either let me go or charge me. Then I'll lawyer up."

"We got a TV watcher here. 'Lawyer up' is quite the Hollywood term, eh? Better call Saul, eh? You watch Breaking Bad?"

"Huh?"

"Nothing."

Detective Green drank back the rest of his coffee and got up from his chair. Smith followed suit.

"We're going to go for the third option."

Marcus wondered what the third option was.

Green opened the door and stepped out of the room. Before closing it, he stuck his head back in the interrogation room and said, "We're going to sweat you."

Then he slammed the door shut.

***

Marcus had no choice but to keep his arms on the table. The waiting was insane. His body shook, his hands fidgeted, and his feet couldn't stay still. His bladder was about to burst. They hadn't offered him a bathroom break since he got there.

He'd yelled a few times, but no one came for him.

This had to be police brutality of some kind. If he had the money, he would have a lawyer here getting him released and having charges laid against those two detectives.

"This is fucking ridiculous," he muttered to himself.

Katy could be anywhere by now. He needed to do something—anything—to find Katy, but instead, he was locked up in interrogation room number two.

Unless he could travel through time and space as he did earlier to escape the bikers.

If he could, he would go to the hospital room and tell his old self to blame everything on Frankie so that the cops would stop looking at him.

If he could convince himself to do that, he would.

Maybe he should call those detectives back in and convince them right here and right now that Frankie was behind everything. Frankie sent bikers to his house, and they abducted Katy.

On second thought, why wasn't he already doing just that?

"Detective Green," he yelled. "I want to talk."

No one came to the door.

"Detective Green!" he shouted.

He listened but heard nothing. No sound of shiny dress shoes coming his way.

They had to have the room miked. There had to be a camera.

Or maybe this was the part of sweating him he wasn't aware of. Wait until he's ready to talk, and then add fifteen minutes to be sure. Or an hour.

What if they didn't come back for a few hours?

He would piss in his pants for sure.

He banged his hands against the table. The cuff on his right wrist caught on the chain and dug into the skin on the side of his wrist. The pain flared up white hot. His eyes watered as he gasped and waited for the pain to subside. He gritted his teeth, placed his feet together under the table, and channeled the pain.

Escaping this room was what was needed. He grunted, moaned, and then screamed, tightening his hands around one another.

He closed his eyes as he shouted and focused on the hospital.

A breeze wafted past his face.

Silence.

He broke his hands apart and opened his eyes.

It worked.

The cuffs were gone. He was sitting on a chair in the waiting room of emergency at the hospital.

"You okay, sir?" a nurse walking by asked. "You had shouted something."

He looked out the windows to his right. The night was an inky black, and yet a moment ago, he was in the interrogation room at noon on a Monday.

"Everything's fine." He looked up at her. When he did, he felt the bandage on his face. "I'm sorry. Just had a sharp pain in my cheek. Nasty cut."

"Are you waiting to go in, or are you just finishing?"

"Waiting for my brother. Do you think I could go in and see him?"

"That depends. I'll look in the system to see if I can locate him. What's his name?"

"Marcus Johnson. He came in with a woman. Her name is Katy."

When he said Katy's name, he couldn't stop his eyes from welling up.

The nurse wrote the names down on a clipboard she was holding. "I'll go check the system. Are you sure you're okay?"

"Yeah." He tried to smile. "Maybe I just need a few more painkillers. I'll be okay, though."

The nurse nodded and stepped away.

He lifted the hood up over his head. He knew exactly where he was and what he needed to do, but if the two detectives who were already talking to him in the cubicle came out this way, he couldn't allow them to see him.

He wondered if he'd get a chance to talk to Katy after he told himself to blame Frankie for the robbery. Maybe he could tell her not to stay at her place that night if he did.

Was there a way he could change the future? Was that what this was all about? Why be given this ability to travel through time and not change what he knew to be a terrible future?

But if he did, and he went back to the future, would he still be in the interrogation room? Would there have been a domestic dispute on his front lawn for the neighbors to call in if he talked Katy into going to a motel with him?

There were too many questions and not enough answers. He had no idea what the ramifications would be if he altered the future by changing the past.

But what he did know was that last night he had visited himself.

So he had to do that, at least. Then decide what to do next.

The nurse opened the door from the area where the emergency patients were tended to. She stuck her head out and held the door open.

"Sir, it looks like your brother is here. Come on. I'll take you to his cubicle."

Marcus got up and followed the nurse inside. He walked by empty cubicles and ones with patients waiting for doctors.

Up ahead, Detectives Smith and Green walked out of his cubicle. As they passed, he kept his face hidden in the hoodie, making sure to keep the nurse between them and him.

They were discussing him. Something about him lying.

Fuck you both, he thought.

The nurse turned and lowered her voice. "He's in there." She pointed.

Marcus pulled the curtain back and stepped inside.

"Who are you?" the Marcus in the bed asked him.

It rattled him to see himself. He wondered if he could even pull this off but knew he'd already done it. He kept most of his face shrouded in the hoodie.

"Tell them," he said in a deeper voice, "that your boss Frankie did this."

"What?" Marcus in the bed asked. "Who are you?"

"This is not important. Tell them you think it was Frankie."

"I know what happened. I'll tell them the truth as I know it. Let me see your face."

"Katy's life depends on this. Don't be a stubborn fool."

Last night's Marcus tried to get up on one elbow at the mention of Katy's name. "How dare you—who are you?"

He moved fast, pushing on the other Marcus's shoulder and shoving him back into the bed.

He clenched his teeth and jaw. "You're not a hero. Don't try to be a tough guy. Just tell them it had to do with Frankie. You're sure of it. The two guys had to have been sent from Frankie. Maybe add that you thought they said his name or something."

"Why would Frankie rob his own store? And how does Katy come into this? And who the fuck are you to know all that?"

"Don't worry about why Frankie would do this or that." Marcus moved toward the opening in the curtain. "Katy comes into this because if you don't do what I've asked, she could be in trouble."

"I'm confused. You're not making sense. How could she be in trouble when I was the one who was robbed? The guys got away. No one involved in this even knows who Katy is."

Marcus pulled his hoodie off, with only the left side of his face aimed at yesterday's Marcus, who leaned back into the pillow so hard he squished it flat.

"Who …?" the Marcus on the bed tried to ask, but his throat caught and closed. He swallowed and tried again. "Who are you?"

"Tell them what I told you. Save Katy." He faced the man in the bed. "For us." A soft luminance flowed past his vision. His return to the current time had begun. "I have to go."

"Wait," yesterday's Marcus said. "What did you mean when you said, 'save Katy for us'?"

Marcus flipped the hoodie back up and ran out.

The detectives were coming. He pivoted and walked the other way.

More lights from the time and place where he was to return came through. He had to locate Katy and warn her. But where did she go when the detectives showed up?

The cafeteria.

He hustled down one hall, then another, following the signs to the cafeteria. What if she walked a different route?

More lights warned him that he was heading back any moment. But where? Back to the interrogation room. He didn't want to go there.

What if he could do it again? Envision where he wanted to go. Would he travel there instead? Wasn't this just another form of bilocation?

As he searched for Katy, he focused on the parking lot in front of his store. He didn't want to travel to another time, just the store.

Get my car. Go see my dad. Find Frankie. Locate Katy.

He turned a corner and saw her.

"Katy!" he called.

She turned a corner up ahead.

The lights brightened around him.

At the second Katy looked back around the corner, he blinked and traveled, and the parking lot surrounded him.

He was sure she had seen him.

Chapter 10

HE HAD A FEW things to consider, and he had to think on them quickly.

First, Katy's safety.

Could he travel back somehow to follow their van? With what? His car was here the whole time. Could he travel back in time inside a vehicle and have the car come with him?

He had a thousand questions for his dad. Whatever he could get out of his father, Marcus needed to know right away. His father wouldn't have called and asked if he had seen himself lately if he didn't know something about the time traveling.

But Katy had to be first.

He checked to make sure no one caught him just showing up in the middle of the parking lot.

It was Monday around lunchtime. The parking lot was relatively full now. He stood between two SUVs, about four vehicles away from his car.

He also had to consider the detectives. Since he was no longer in their interrogation room and had no plans to return, they would be out looking for him.

They hadn't arrested him, but leaving their custody without

permission would probably not be good. Whatever trouble that brought, he could deal with after finding Katy and ensuring she was okay.

At his car door, he pulled on the handle.

His heart sank.

The door was locked.

Of course, it's locked.

His keys were on the night table by his side of the bed back at the house.

"Shit."

Now what?

He turned toward the front of the store, The Act of Love. The neon open sign was off. As far as he could tell, the lights on the inside were also off, although the sun's glare on the window made it difficult to be sure.

Inside the store, a man peeked out through the glass.

Marcus recognized him immediately. The biker who chased him around the house with the gun in his hand.

He broke out in a cold sweat, and his hands shook. He lowered his head to remain unseen. He needed a plan. Could he fight them one on one? He didn't have a weapon.

The knife.

It was still behind the store in the bushes.

Perfect.

He waited until the store's window was clear for more than fifteen seconds, then stepped from behind the SUV and walked away. He headed to the end of the strip mall, where he would come around to the back of the store that way.

If the biker was hiding out in the store, Katy might be with him. It was perfect. Everything was coming together seamlessly. He understood their reasoning. They wanted Marcus. Marcus's car was parked out front. At some time, he would come for his car. It was parked where someone could watch the car from behind the counter inside the store. He parked it so he could watch it when he was working.

But they had made a mistake. They had shown themselves a few seconds too early. They hadn't kept their cards close to their chest. If he hadn't seen the biker, he might've walked right up to the window to look inside to see if Frankie was there.

But not now. No, now he was coming in the back door, and he would be armed.

Let's see what they make of that.

He walked past the coffee shop, the dry cleaners, the massage studio, and finally, the convenience store at the end of the long building. At the corner, he turned cautiously, just in case, and continued along the side of the complex until he reached the back.

At the back, a thin road spanned the length of the strip mall all the way to the other end. It was lined with garbage dumpsters on one side and small steps leading to the back of each business. No cars, and no one was standing around watching the back of The Act of Love.

He crossed the road and hopped onto the little grassy area where the bushes started. He stayed behind the store's dumpsters as much as possible in case someone was watching the back.

As he neared the rear of Frankie's store, he flanked the edge of the bushes, prepared to jump in and grab the knife if anyone surprised him.

A soft breeze brushed at his hair, the midday sun high. He wiped the sweat from his brow.

What was he doing? How had his life descended into a hole so fast?

What was happening to him that he could travel through time by thought? Wasn't bilocation when he was in two places at once? If that was the case, and he wasn't in the interrogation room anymore, then he wasn't bilocating.

Unless being in that hospital room a few minutes ago, in two places at one time, was bilocation.

He decided it had to be time travel. As he ran away from a biker at his house earlier, he had traveled to the store's parking lot the previous night. That was a different time and place.

He had traveled back a few times but never forward. Whenever the current time pulled him back, which it seemed to do naturally on its own, it took about a minute to complete the process. But now he knew he could go to a different place before that process was completed. Or would the future fix things and eventually draw him back to the interrogation room?

He tried to banish the thoughts. This wasn't the time or place. He had to get inside the store to see if Katy was there. One step at a time.

At the back of the store, yellow police tape billowed softly in the breeze. It was wrapped around the back steps and railing, but the back door was closed.

The garbage bags he had dropped by the garbage bin were gone, no doubt placed inside the dumpster.

The police must've finished their investigation while he was being stitched up. Someone had cleaned everything up except for the police tape.

He stood directly behind the door, marking the spot where he threw the knife. Pivoting on his heels, he stared down at the bushes.

A door opened behind him.

"Turn around," a male voice said. "No hero stuff."

Shit.

He had come so close to getting the knife. Even if he saw it, he couldn't go for it now. The knife would be taken, and he would be no better off than he was now.

"I said, turn around. Last chance."

Marcus raised his hands above his waist and slowly turned around to face the biker who stood on the store's back steps, a gun in one hand.

The biker had a large smile pasted on his mug. He laughed for a moment and wiped his face. "You have to tell me. How stupid are you?"

"Excuse me?"

"How stupid are you that you would return to the crime scene?"

"Coming to work. I work Mondays. This is my shift."

"Then what are you doing sneaking around the building and standing by the bushes if you were coming to open the store?"

Marcus smiled back at him. "Looking for clues. Maybe the idiots who robbed me left something behind the police missed."

"The idiots who robbed you, eh?"

Marcus wondered if his stomach would ever feel the same. Everywhere he turned, everything he had done since last night had been nerve-wracking. And now a crazy biker was pointing a gun at him.

If the biker raised the gun and it looked like he was going to shoot, Marcus would have to disappear.

"Where did you go this morning? You were gone when I followed you around the corner of the house." He raised a finger in the air. "I was three seconds behind you. It was impossible to hide anywhere at that time. So where did you go?"

Nothing he said would be believable, so he went for the truth.

"I disappeared into thin air and traveled back through time. If you'd have waited ten to fifteen minutes, you would've seen me come back."

The biker's face hardened, and his jaw muscles flexed as he clenched his teeth.

"You want to play me for a fool? Who do you think I am? I'm the guy holding the gun." He raised it and gestured in a rolling motion. "Get over here."

Marcus started walking, got to the stairs, and started up them, wishing he had gotten to the knife.

At the top of the stairs, they stood at eye level. The biker kept his weapon trained on Marcus the whole time.

"Where's Katy?" Marcus asked.

"Get inside."

Once inside, the biker closed the door behind him.

"In the office," the biker said. "Go. Now."

Marcus took in the back room. The table where he ate his lunch, the ruined safe under the counter, and the mess of footsteps on the dustier part of the floor from all the traffic stomping in and out since last night.

He entered Frankie's office. The ruined door lay broken up and cracked on the floor.

The store was empty except for the two of them. He faced the biker and lowered his hands.

"Where's Katy?"

The biker walked behind Frankie's desk and sat without answering. He placed the gun on the desk calendar, the barrel aimed at Marcus, a finger inside the trigger guard.

"Where's the money?" the biker asked.

"Excuse me?"

"Where's the money? That's the last time I ask that question."

Marcus had never so much as even seen a gun other than on TV. He'd never met hardened men like the biker and didn't know what made them tick. All he knew was that nothing would scare or intimidate a man like the one sitting in Frankie's chair. At least nothing is coming from a guy like Marcus.

But the one thing he did know was that he could disappear on a moment's notice if things went south. That meant he had nothing to lose.

He pushed one of the two guest chairs, so it faced the biker and sat down.

"We'll do a question for a question," he said. "Deal?"

The biker's smile made him look like a lunatic.

"I don't think so," Biker said. "I ask, you answer. That's it."

Marcus steepled his hands and lowered his head. "You want information but won't get it if I'm dead. I'll answer your questions if you answer mine. Otherwise," he met the biker's eyes. "Go fuck yourself."

The biker raised the gun, cocked the hammer, and pointed it at Marcus.

For a second, Marcus thought he was going to shoot. In that second, he thought about the back bushes. What a great place to travel. Grab the knife, and he could finish him off when the biker ran out the back door.

But the gun didn't go off, and Marcus didn't disappear.

The biker slowly lowered the weapon back to the desk.

Marcus took a deep breath and tightened his grip on the arms of the chair to hide the shaking in his hands. His bladder almost gave out at that moment as he wondered if he could travel out of the room faster than a speeding bullet.

"Katy is in hiding," the biker said.

"That's not an answer," Marcus said.

"Where's the money?"

"In hiding."

"Okay, this isn't working." The biker turned toward the monitor and flicked it on. He looked at Marcus over his shoulder. "Maybe this'll help you open up."

He touched a couple of dials on the digital video recorder. From where Marcus sat, it looked like he was adjusting the video saved on the hard drive to a certain time.

The screen was split in four, each camera trained on its respective spot in the store.

"This shot is right after you walked into the back of the store last night," Biker said, pointing at the camera with his finger. "Recognize it?"

Marcus leaned forward and saw himself in the back room on the phone.

"Yeah, my dad called me."

"Now watch this."

He twisted a dial that sped the feed up. Just as Marcus took the garbage out and then ran by the back room camera before entering this office to turn the power to the cameras off, the biker stopped the feed.

He faced Marcus, that evil smile on his face again. "Here's why you're so stupid. You think Frankie would leave his store unguarded in any way? If so, you don't know Frankie very well. Actually, you don't know Frankie at all. You think he owns this store, don't you?" Biker shook his head. "Man, are you ever fucking stupid."

Marcus's brain was racing. Didn't Frankie own the store? Wasn't he the boss? If not, then who?

The biker flipped a switch, and the monitor's screen displayed two new cameras. Marcus stood to study the screens closer. He had never seen these cameras.

One showed the back door all the way to the garbage, a circular shape to the video image from a dome lens. The other showed the front of the safe and surrounding area, with Marcus in clear view as he pried the safe open.

Marcus needed to sit down. His legs went weak. He couldn't believe Frankie hadn't told him about the other cameras in the entire two years he'd worked there.

Who could really be trusted? Even your most long-standing employee couldn't be.

But now what?

"What we're all trying to figure out was," the Biker paused as he pointed to the edge of the screen, "who is that?"

Someone was with Marcus in the back room.

Marcus watched in utter fascination. He had no idea who it was. He had been alone. No doubt about it. He wondered if he was losing his mind.

The biker started the camera again. After Marcus returned from stashing the money in the car, he walked off the back camera and disappeared for twelve seconds. Then he reappeared to answer his phone and lay down on the floor.

"That's it until the police arrive. The other person doesn't show up again. But I think you took care of that other person when you were off camera."

Marcus was speechless.

"We already guessed you stashed the cash in your car," the biker continued. "I checked it out. The glove box, the door panel, the trunk, maybe new holes drilled out for hiding places, but the money wasn't there. Not even in that tennis ball container under the seat. I couldn't find a thing except for all that blood in the back seat. Any idea whose that is?" He slammed the gun down on the desk. "So, where's the money?" He tapped the gun on the desk again for effect.

Blood on the back seat? No money in the tennis ball container? Impossible.

What the hell is going on?

Marcus was done. He had lost. It was over. He would apologize, deal with the detectives, and serve his time. It was a first offense. Maybe they would go lightly on him. But where was the money?

Whose blood was in his car, and who was with him last night? It wasn't himself going back in time because the shoulders of the other person were slimmer and more feminine in their softness and angle. No way it was him—

"Hey!" the biker screamed, knocking him out of his thoughts.

He looked up and met the biker's eyes.

"I'll tell you everything," Marcus said. "But I want Katy back." Then he added, "Unharmed."

"Too late."

Like he was plugged into an electrical outlet, his heart rate spiked, and his body filled with adrenaline. He had a sudden urge to dive across the desk, gun or no gun, and strangle the biker. At least it would erase that insane smile on his face.

In a controlled voice, he asked, "What does that mean?"

"She had an accident. But we'll talk about that later. There's something more important to talk about right now."

"Explain to me what would be more important to me than Katy?" He sat forward. "Because I'm about done with you until I see Katy alive and well."

The biker clicked the gun again. Marcus was about to yell at him to stop fiddling with the gun like it was a toy.

"How about a blowtorch?" the biker asked. "Pliers? Maybe a hammer and nails?"

"What the hell are you talking about?"

"The tools of torture, asshole."

If they had used any of that on Katy, he would murder every last one of these people.

"I know what you're thinking," the biker said. "But Katy wasn't touched."

Marcus breathed deeply.

"But if you don't tell me what I want to know, my men will enjoy themselves using as many tools on you as they can, extracting information from you for weeks."

Marcus leaned back in the chair and sat in a normal position. For now, he would play it their way. Unless he wanted to disappear, he needed to hear what this man had to say about Katy. He had nowhere to go next. The police would be looking for him. Frankie knew without a doubt that he had robbed his store. It was over, truly over, before it even had a chance to begin.

"If Frankie doesn't own the store, who does?" Marcus asked.

"Call them a consortium. They own over fifty stores in Ontario alone. To pay back favors, people like Frankie are sold as the frontman. But Frankie got into a spot of trouble about a year ago. He couldn't be trusted. Extra cameras were installed. He had to spend weekends in jail for the last eleven months. During that time, he was left alone as long as the store stayed open and produced results. But we were tasked to keep an eye on it while he was away." The biker tapped the top of the monitor. "This DVR is accessible through the internet. I was in my hotel room watching you use the crowbar on the safe. The police beat me here. Otherwise, you would have been dead last night."

Marcus didn't know if he was bluffing or not. None of it mattered, though. He needed to leave before this madman shot him or worse.

"Now that you know you worked for some real bad dudes," he said like he was talking to a baby, "aren't you pissed that Frankie wasn't honest with you?"

"I'm only pissed about two things."

"Oh yeah, what's that?"

"I'm pissed that you won't tell me where Katy is and if she's okay, and I'm pissed that you're holding a gun on me."

"Katy didn't make it."

Marcus's world shattered with those words.

"Nasty bump on the head." The biker got up from the chair and walked around the desk, hovering over Marcus. "Who knew it would hit her temple that hard? She bled out on the front doorstep of your house. Crazy, huh?"

Marcus's thoughts spun. He began to hyperventilate. Could Katy really be gone? Did they kill her? It couldn't be true. He refused to believe it. This was some ploy to get him to break down and tell them everything. No one killed someone over three thousand dollars. Especially someone who wasn't even involved in the crime. He was the one who robbed the safe. They couldn't have done it. No way.

"I can take you to her body. How's that sound?" The biker leaned down and whispered in his ear, "One last kiss?"

Marcus shot out of his chair, knocking the gun from the biker's grasp. By the time he was fully standing, the biker had an arm around Marcus's throat. His windpipe closed from the pressure. His eyes bulged as he flailed at the arm.

The biker yanked downward, pulling him toward the floor, but Marcus focused on his bedroom. He focused hard, envisioned it, smelled the familiar smell, and almost tasted it.

When he shut his eyes, he was there, in his bedroom, the covers still ruffled from that morning when he left the bed to have a bath.

His throat opened. His starving lungs gasped in a full shot of air. He opened his eyes.

Traveling through space and time was getting easier.

He shook himself off and fell back onto the bed, breathing heavily, his stomach sick, his bladder screaming for release.

After a minute of breathing to calm down, he got up on wobbly legs and walked to the bathroom.

When he had relieved himself, he stumbled back to the edge of the tub and covered his mouth with his hand.

How could that be?

Blood covered the floor and the mat under the bathroom sink, his fresh footprints imprinted.

How did I miss it just now? What's happening to me? Or did this happen after I left this morning?

He ran from the bathroom, grabbed his car keys, and walked down to the kitchen, where he grabbed a loaf of bread. He needed something to absorb the acids roiling around in his stomach.

At the front door, he slipped on his running shoes without bothering to clean the blood off his feet. He opened the bag of bread and bit into a piece. Outside the front door, he stepped into the dried pool of Katy's blood.

Yellow police tape encircled his front step and walkway.

When did this happen?

He ducked under the police tape and started up the street. His father lived ten blocks away.

He would get there before two in the afternoon. They would talk before his father had much of a chance to get too drunk, and he would get the answers he needed.

Then he would travel back in time to the night before the robbery and talk himself out of doing it.

That would fix everything, and Katy would still be alive. The bikers would have never been in his life, and the two detectives wouldn't even know his name. He would quit his job on Tuesday when Frankie was scheduled to return and be done with it.

All these people, the police included, would be out of his life as if they had never been there in the first place. He would get another job, and they'd be okay.

Everything would be okay.

He thought about what his father had asked him as he walked and ate dry pieces of bread.

Have I ever seen myself?

What the hell did that mean?

Chapter 11

THE GRASS WAS UNKEMPT, brown, and brittle. The front of the house needed a paint job. Flakes of eggshell-white paint peeled in spots around the old windows that should've been replaced in the seventies.

His father never had the money to fix the house up. It all went into booze.

Marcus stopped at the small iron gate and contemplated his father's death. He was in his late fifties. Under other circumstances, his father had a couple of decades left, but the booze had pared down those years. Marcus would be surprised if his father could make it ten more years.

The gate creaked as he opened it. The latch clicked with a solid thud behind him as the gate swung back on a strong spring. The three-story Victorian loomed over him as he walked up the path. Marcus kept an eye on the windows for movement.

The road had been quiet on the way over. Vigilant to stay off the radar, he had watched for roaming police cars or Harley-Davidsons.

If what the biker had told him in Frankie's office was true, then nothing could help Katy but going back in time. Once he was done with his father, he would focus his attention on the night of the robbery and head back. He could still fix everything.

One talk with good old Dad, and everything would return to normal.

When he knocked on the front door, he thought about going back ten years to talk to his father about his drinking problem. Maybe he could make routine visits to his old man and curb his habits enough to save his life.

He knocked again, then rang the bell.

Don't tell me you've already passed out.

"Round here," his father yelled from the back of the house.

Marcus frowned.

He's outside? The only time he goes out is to get more booze.

He jumped off the front steps, crossed the weed-covered lawn, and rounded the side of the house.

Christmas was more than six months ago. The area had been covered in snow and ice then. Now that it was mid-summer and the foliage was exposed, Marcus had no idea how bad the old man's yard had gotten. If Marcus had the money, he would hire a landscaping company to clear everything out and fix it up. It was so bad he had to wonder why the city hadn't sent his father a letter forcing him to clean it up yet.

The shed in the back needed as much paint as the house. He scanned the yard and followed the path to the back steps and the back door without seeing his father anywhere.

"Right here." An arm rose from behind a row of hedges, then dropped back out of sight. "What can I help you with?"

Worried, he wondered what his father was doing back there, lying around in the bushes. Didn't he recognize his only son?

Then his father's head popped up, and Marcus got another surprise.

Dad looked good. His weathered face glowed with a healthy

radiance, his smile bright. For a brief moment, he wondered if he had traveled back in time to fifteen years earlier without even knowing it. Or maybe his father had been the one who had traveled.

"Son, it's been too long. So good to see you."

Marcus was lost for words.

His father slapped his hands together a few times to rid them of dirt. "Come on in the house. Let me wash up, and we'll have coffee or something."

His father stepped out from behind the bush and started for the house. Marcus followed.

They entered the mud room at the back. The washer and dryer were brand new, and the sink was clean.

What's going on?

None of this was like his father.

"I'm so happy you took my call the other night." His father untied and removed his shoes. When he stood, a tear sat in the corner of his eye. "I've missed you, Marcus. But I wanted to wait to make sure it was definite."

"What was definite?" Marcus asked, finding his voice.

"We'll talk in the living room."

His father headed down the hall toward the bathroom.

"I thought maybe you'd call first," he said over his shoulder. "But an impromptu visit works for me."

The bathroom door shut, and the sink turned on.

Marcus's dad hadn't asked about the bandage on his face yet, but he would soon enough. Marcus left his shoes on to cover his bloodstained feet as he left the mud room and turned for the living room. Under the alcove to the living room, he stopped. Everything was new and shiny. The house had been redone from top to bottom in the previous six months. Nothing was recognizable. The furniture could've been featured in an interior design magazine. Either his father had just won the lottery and hired a designer, or this wasn't his father's house anymore.

He was afraid to step on the new plush carpet. Even the hallway's wooden floor was freshly waxed.

He entered the kitchen, where he could stay on the tile floor until his father returned.

The kitchen had a new table and chairs. Even the appliances on the counter were new. A Breville juicer sat beside a shiny silver espresso machine. A large KitchenAid sat on its own table in the corner.

What the hell is going on here? Juicing?

Marcus ran to the front door and looked through the peephole. The street beyond was empty. No police cars and no motorcycles.

He hustled back to the kitchen, pulled out one of the chairs, and sat down. He bounced his leg up and down and bit his lower lip while waiting.

Come on, Dad. Explain all this shit.

The sink in the bathroom turned off.

Footsteps approached from down the hall. His dad walked past the kitchen door and stopped in the living room.

"Where'd you go?"

"Kitchen."

A second later, his dad entered the kitchen with a wide smile. "Why here? Come sit in the living room."

"Dirty feet. Can't take my shoes off."

His dad nodded and looked down at his shoes. When he looked back up, he said, "You like what I've done with the place?"

"What's going on, Dad?"

"Whatever could you mean?"

Then he bowed, extended his arms, and wore a hideous smile as if he had just finished a stellar performance as the lead in a popular stage show.

"Seriously, Dad. What happened here? Where did you get all this stuff?"

His father moved to the espresso machine, where he pushed buttons and flicked switches.

"Dad, I don't want coffee," Marcus said with more bite in his voice than he intended. "I want to talk."

His father stopped and leaned against the counter, his arms crossed. "What happened to your face?"

"Accident. What's going on here?"

"That looks like a big accident."

"I'll tell you about it later."

A moment of silence passed between them. They eyed each other, suspicious after years of lies and deceit.

Last Christmas had been a one-off. Marcus decided to come to see him over the holidays because he was sure his father wouldn't live too much longer.

He decided he would wait his father out. He wasn't going to talk first.

"I'm sober."

"For real this time?" Marcus asked.

His father didn't move or speak.

"How long?"

"January ten is my dry date."

"Dry date?"

"The day I stopped drinking. The day I dried up." He chuckled. "Can't you tell? Don't I look great?"

He extended his arms and spun in a circle like he was high on some hallucinogenic drug. He always had a flamboyant way about him, but he hadn't shown it like this in years. If the man hadn't been married to Marcus's mother and shown an interest in women in the past, he would've thought his father was gay.

"The other night when you called," Marcus stopped to swallow. His mouth was dry from all the dry bread he had eaten on the way over. "You sounded drunk."

"I was emotional. I wasn't drunk. Not a drop of alcohol in this body since early January. Aren't you happy for your Pops?"

"Of course," Marcus said. It was hard to be filled with joy at the moment with how chaotic his life had become. Until he went back in time to fix everything, Katy would remain dead. Nothing would make him happy while Katy rotted. "How did you get all this new stuff?"

"Bought it."

"With what money?" Marcus asked.

"Oh, Son, you don't know much about me anymore, do you?" His father walked over to the table and took a seat opposite him. "I didn't spend any of the money I got from the life insurance because of your mother's death so I could help you when the time came. The interest had ballooned over the years. I used that money to fix things up. The only room I didn't touch was your old room."

"Why all the changes?"

"Since I was reborn," he winked twice and smiled that quirky smile, "I couldn't keep living the way I was with the memories of your mother. I know it's been twenty years, but some get over things quicker than others. I still tear up when our song comes on."

"I remember it. That one from, The Hollies."

His father nodded. "Long Cool Woman in a Black Dress." He looked down at his hands, rolling his fingers around. "That's the one." He looked back up. "I changed on the inside first. Then I changed on the outside. I decided to do that on the house. The interior is all done and healed. Now I'm starting on the outside. You caught me in the new garden. Next is the yard and the shrubs up front. By September, I'm repainting the shed and the front of the house in time for winter. My goal is to have everything done before the snow falls. We'll have an alcohol-free Christmas this year. How does that sound? Would Katy mind?"

Marcus swallowed hard and looked away for a moment so as not to alert his father with his expression at the mention of Katy's name.

"You two are still together, right?"

Marcus nodded. "When you called, you said some weird stuff. That's why I thought you'd been drinking. What was that about 'seeing myself'?"

"Wait here."

His father got up and walked down the hall. A door opened and closed. It gave Marcus a chance to check the front of the house again. Through the peephole, nothing moved on the street.

He breathed a sigh of relief and headed back to the kitchen table.

A moment later, his father returned. He held a small black book with a lock. He set it on the table and slid the key across to Marcus.

"What's this?" Marcus asked. "A diary?"

"Of sorts."

"Whose?"

"Your mother's."

Marcus picked it up and examined the leather cover, the strap, and the tiny lock. "What do you want me to do with it?" Marcus asked.

"Read it."

"Isn't there personal stuff in here? I barely knew her. I was only eight when she had the accident."

His father shook his head.

"What?"

"It wasn't a car accident."

He didn't know how many revelations he could handle in one day. Either his father was lying again, or Marcus suffered from his Early Onset Alzheimer's. Nothing added up or made sense. He was afraid his reality was about to shift, and he would never be the same again.

"What are you talking about?" he asked cautiously.

"In your mother's will, she instructed that you got this book and the key when you turned eighteen."

"Why am I just getting it now?"

"That's my fault, and I'm sorry." His father reached across the table to touch his arm. "I was too drunk in those days. By the time you turned eighteen and moved out, giving you a book was the last thing on my mind. When I was cleaning the house out, getting rid of the old, and preparing for the new, I found it."

Marcus sat up straighter. "Have you read it?"

His father shook his head. "I would never violate your mother's privacy. I respect her memory too much. I wallowed in my selfishness for too long. From here on in, I will respect her by living better for you and me."

Marcus looked at the book and turned it over in his hands.

"What did you mean on the phone?" he asked.

"I think you'll understand everything better once you read what she has written in there."

Marcus narrowed his eyes. "How would you know that if you haven't read it?"

"Because I suspect what she wrote to you is about what happened to her."

"I was eight when I last saw her. So tell me, what happened to her?"

"You know she had the Early Onset Alzheimer's, right?"

Marcus nodded.

"Did you know she was also a scientist working with the Toronto University on experiments in particle acceleration?"

"Particle acceleration?"

"They were attempting to move particles faster than the speed of light. As far as I know, they weren't successful. But your mother discovered something else."

"So you have read this?" Marcus held the book up.

"Marcus, you can stop asking me that. I haven't read what is on those pages, but I think it'll have something to do with bilocation. When she was alive, she confided in me."

"Do you mean time travel?" Marcus asked.

He studied his father's face for any sign that he was surprised by the words "time travel." Not even a tick under the eye. Nothing.

"Time travel," his father repeated. "It's probably all in there."

Marcus set the book down beside the tiny key, astounded. Was he really sitting in his father's newly decorated home and discussing time travel? Three nights ago, he was at work in the adult store selling lotions, creams, and marital aids, and now he was talking to his father about altering the time and space continuum.

"Before I read what Mom wanted to say to me, tell me what you know."

"I don't know much. Most of what your mother worked on was confidential."

"Give me what you do have. It could mean the difference between life and death."

His father frowned but didn't ask what he meant.

"I've never told anyone this. Outside this house, I will deny it."

Marcus nodded and leaned forward, his interest piqued.

"Your mother and I flew to Paris a year before you were born. We stayed a week and flew back. One of the best trips of our marriage." His face clouded over as the memories flooded back. "The day before we were to leave, a woman showed up at our hotel and rang our room. Your mother said it was someone from the university and for me to stay in the room."

"What happened? Who was it?"

"After she left our room, I took the stairs to see who she was meeting. When I got to the lobby, I couldn't believe what I was seeing."

Marcus had leaned forward, his chest pushing on the table. "What?" he asked.

"Your mother was talking to … your mother."

"Huh?"

"It was like I was staring at her twin. They were even in the same clothes."

"What were they talking about?"

"I have no idea. I ran back up the stairs and waited in the room for her to return. When she did, she told me we had to change our flights and return sooner. We argued. I wanted to know why tomorrow wasn't soon enough. We packed that afternoon and flew out of Paris that night."

"Did you ever find out why you had to cut your vacation short or who that other woman was?"

His father nodded slowly.

Marcus waited.

The look in his father's eyes convinced him that what he was about to hear would change him forever. His father's forehead loosened, and the wrinkles of strain touched the crow's feet at the edge of each eye.

"It *was* your mother visiting your mother. She had come from the future to warn us of the impending plane crash that would kill us. We changed planes and made it home safely. The plane we were originally booked on crashed. Almost all on board were killed."

Ripples of goosebumps rolled up Marcus's arms.

"Neither one of you thought to tell the airline? Doesn't that make you partly responsible?"

"You're joking, right? How could we walk up to Air France's counter and say we saw the future? Or better yet, came back from the future and could see what would happen? They would blame us. They would think we were responsible once the plane went down. No, this had to stay with us."

Marcus fingered the small book, wondering what was written inside its pages.

"Your mother opened up to me about the experiments after that. Even though I wasn't cleared at her level, she needed someone to talk to."

"So, what killed her if it wasn't a car accident?"

"I said it wasn't an *accident*, as in by chance. She was in the car when it hit that pickup truck, and she died, but it wasn't an *accident*."

"You're talking in circles."

"No." He shook his head. "What I'm saying is that it was intentional."

"What? Intentional? Why? How?"

"Your mother was involved in experiments that allowed her to alter matter and change her whereabouts by thought alone. She did these experiments and allowed them to inject her with whatever they had concocted. The tests proved successful in her trials. The problem was, she didn't know she was pregnant with you when she did this. It wasn't until you were almost three months along before she realized you were in her womb."

"What does all this mean for me?" He tried hard to appear stunned.

"When you were born, she was devastated, worried that she had hurt her baby with all that she had been involved in, but you came out looking normal and acting normal. She swore that if she were responsible for you having some kind of deformity, she wouldn't be able to live with herself."

"Are you saying I can bilocate by thought, too?" he asked, hoping his shocked look was believable. Inside, he was elated to discover he wasn't losing his mind.

His father nodded and got up to pace the kitchen. "You disappeared once when you were in the living room with her. She had no idea where you had gone. One minute you were sitting on the couch crying because you had broken the window in the back with a soccer ball, and the next minute, you were gone. She waited fifteen minutes in a panic until you showed up again. She blamed herself for everything."

Wanting to get off the topic of him traveling, he asked, "What's intentional about a car accident?"

"Your mother got quieter in the last few months before her death. Stopped talking to people, stopped talking to me, but doted on you. You became her new project. In her worst moments, she read the news, searching for something. Always searching for something." He wiped at his eyes. "On the other side of the city, a manhunt had begun for a felon on the loose who had raped and killed three teenage girls."

"What did that have to do with our family?"

"Your mother had a weird sense of justice. She felt that if she righted another major wrong, she could be forgiven for wronging you."

Marcus understood. "So she traveled back in time with the name of the man the police were looking for, found him, and ran into him before he could touch those girls? Is that what you're telling me?"

His father stopped pacing. "It's times like this when I could really use a drink."

Marcus got up and walked to the front door. It had been too long since he had last checked. He needed to keep his head in the game and stay sharp, or he would never be able to save Katy.

When he was done traveling back in time, the police wouldn't even know his name anymore. He was so close to fixing everything he could taste it. It would all go away and go back to normal. In a way, he was doing what his father did. Clean up the inside and then fix his exterior life.

His father had followed him out of the kitchen.

"What's going on?" he asked. "Why so jumpy? Is what we're talking about disturbing you?"

Marcus turned around. "Katy said she'd pick me up. Just looking for her car." He was surprised at how fast the lie came out. "Maybe I'll just walk home."

"Heard enough already?"

"No, no, it's just, it's a lot to take in. A lot to think about."

"I understand. Now that I'm sober, I'd love to have you and the missus over for dinner one night." He stepped in closer. "I really miss you, Son."

"I miss you, too, Dad." He wrapped his arms around his father and held him for a moment. "Good job on being sober. I'm proud of you."

"Thanks."

They held a moment longer, then let go and stepped back.

"Well, I better get that book and head home to read what Mom wanted to tell me."

"You do that."

In the kitchen, his father started on the espresso machine again.

"You sure you don't want one before you leave?"

"I'm sure."

Marcus stopped at the kitchen door.

"Dad?"

"Yeah?"

"At Christmas, you regaled us with stories of my particular brand of hide and go seek. Was any of that true?"

"I don't remember what I said at Christmas. I do remember drinking myself into a coma, though."

"You said I would disappear from one room and reappear in

another. I brushed it off as hide and go seek. But was that me using my power? The power Mom passed down to me."

He turned to face him. "Marcus, you would disappear a lot in those days. When your mother died, you stopped. I thought it was gone, so we never talked about it."

"How did Mom feel about me having this ability? I mean, from what you said, she blamed herself, but is there anything else you can tell me?"

"Not really …"

"You know what this sounds like?" Marcus asked.

His father took a tentative step toward him.

"Mom's guilt for doing those experiments while pregnant and passing on whatever it was she passed to me caused her to kill herself after she realized that I could travel through time as well."

"Now, Marcus—"

"Dad, I had no idea Mom killed herself because of me." His eyes watered up. Another nail in his emotional coffin.

How can I live with this?

"And now Katy is dead because of me. I'm a real lady killer."

He ran for the mud room and the door to the backyard, his father on his tail, asking him what he meant about Katy.

When he got outside, he clutched the book tight to his chest and focused hard on last week.

It was time to go back and fix everything.

But nothing happened.

He tried again as his father crowded him on the back walkway by the garden, shouting Katy's name in his ear.

Still, nothing happened.

What's happening?

"Dad, be quiet," he shouted back. "I can't concentrate."

The sound of a police siren in the distance was enough for Marcus to realize that he needed to get as far away from his father's house as possible.

He needed to get to his car.

Then he could drive somewhere secluded and read his mom's book.

Maybe his mother left him a manual on how to use his ability.

He ran through his father's backyard, hopped the fence, and landed hard on the other side.

He rolled onto his back, scrunched up his face at the pain, and gasped for air.

When he opened his eyes, he was in the parking lot of his store.

And the biker was rifling through the back seat of his car.

He had traveled back to a time before he arrived at the store and fought with the biker in Frankie's office. Back to when the biker searched Marcus's car for the money.

His earlier self hadn't met with the biker yet.

Now he had the advantage.

Now it was time to make things right.

Chapter 12

Detective Green sat at the back of the café across from the police station and opened his files, spreading them out on the small table. His partner joined him with a coffee in one hand and a panini in the other.

"What have we got?" Detective Smith asked as he sat across from Green.

"Well, I can tell you what we don't have," Green said. "A body."

"Yeah, but we have everything else."

"I know. The arrest warrant for Marcus Johnson has already been signed."

"Why did it take so long?"

"That last case, we fucked up. A duck likes water. A fish swims." He shrugged. "Who knows why the Crown Attorney dithers on this shit? The great mystery of our time."

"Okay," Smith said. He bit into his sandwich. With a mouth full, he mumbled, "Calm down." After a few bites, he swallowed. "Where's our man Marcus Johnson now?"

"Last known location was his father's house."

"Our officers get there in time?"

Green shook his head and took the chance to sip his coffee.

"Marcus jumped the back fence and disappeared. His father is being brought in for questioning."

"Fuckin' A. The threat of charges like harboring a fugitive will get him talking."

Green snickered. "He's talking just fine, last I heard."

"How the hell did this get so fucked up?"

"No idea, but I think we added to it."

"How's that?" Smith asked, ripping into his panini.

"After watching the camera feed from Frankie's store again, I caught the image of a woman standing just out of view. It looked like she was waiting for Marcus to finish work."

Smith's eyebrows rose. His mouth was too full to talk.

Green continued, "It looks like a neighbor has come forward and swears a member of the Spawns Motorcycle Club—identified by the jacket on one of the men—was seen in the area of Marcus's house earlier, but we can't confirm they are involved. Except that Marcus's neighbor, the one who called about the domestic at his place, mentioned seeing two men on his front lawn and a black van out front. We know the Spawns use black vans."

"True, but how is there so much blood at Marcus's house? We located the weapon in the bushes behind the store Marcus worked at. The blood matches Katy's. The only prints on the knife were Marcus's."

Smith jumped in, "The blood all over Marcus's house was Katy's, too. Even the blood in the bathroom."

"So tell me," Green said. "What's your theory? Happy-go-lucky Marcus robbed his own store and killed his woman? Then drove her body to his house where she bled out some more?"

"That would explain the blood in his car."

"Neighbors will say that Marcus loved Katy. I suspect they'll say the same thing when we find his friends."

"Who knows why people kill each other," Smith said. He wiped his mouth with a napkin. "All we've got is the store was robbed. Katy's blood is at the scene, on the knife with Marcus's prints, and all over their house. Marcus has a gash on his cheek. And he's run from us and continues to evade capture." He clucked his tongue. "Doesn't look good for Marcus. His best option is to come in and explain himself."

Green nodded. "Who knew that fucking door was still defective and didn't lock on the interrogation room? And how did he get out of those handcuffs? That's what I want to know." He drifted off for a second, lost in thought. "I still can't believe he ran from the cop shop." He drank from his coffee.

"No one saw him," Smith said. "How the hell did he pull that off? We even checked the interrogation room cameras. Nothing. One minute he's there, the camera seems to blip, and then Marcus is gone. What, did the guy just disappear?"

"No idea, but whatever he did had to be some kind of magic because those cuffs have been used on some of the toughest guys. Little Marcus didn't even break them."

"Do you think Frankie had anything to do with any of this?" Smith asked.

"From weekend jail? I'm sure he could, but nothing points at Frankie except that this is his area of expertise, and the Spawns are known associates."

"I follow evidence like a hound. Come on, Green, you know me. Speculation is for lawyers. We've got an arrest warrant. And don't we also have a search warrant for his car now, too?"

"Yeah, a crime scene crew was sent to the store as well as the car."

"I'm sure we'll get to the bottom of this within a day or so. We'll see that this fuckin' guy is a murderer, and the case will be sewn up. Done. Next. Off to another case."

Smith bit into the second half of his panini.

"Sometimes you're a dick, you know that?"

"What?" he said with a mouthful. "What'd I say?"

"Just eat up. We should be at the house in case Marcus returns. We still have to find Katy's body, and I don't think it's far from the house with the amount of blood found there."

Green's phone rang. He flipped it open.

"Detective Green here."

"Hey, it's Larry down at the Act Of Love store. Marcus Johnson just showed up on the street out front."

"We've got the arrest warrant with us. Grab him."

"Okay. I'm on it."

Green hung up. "Come on, Smith. They got Marcus at the store. Let's roll."

Smith grunted in protest but got up, crumbs falling from his chin.

Green turned back. He'd almost forgotten his coffee in the excitement.

Chapter 13

MARCUS EDGED AROUND A vehicle on his hands and knees for a better view of the man rummaging around in the back seat of his car.

It wasn't the biker. Whoever it was appeared to be dusting something with a brush.

The store's interior lights were bright, illuminating a dozen or so men in white suits. One man stood out among the others. He was at the front window, his hand holding a cell phone to his ear.

The man stared directly at Marcus.

Shit.

He had to forget about the car. There would be no retrieving it now. He could never return to the store. Something was going on that was bigger than him. He didn't understand it, but none of that mattered anymore. He didn't have to understand anything.

All he needed to do was figure out what his mother wanted to tell him in the book she left for him and then travel back a few days to right all the wrongs.

He walked with purpose through the parking lot.

He glanced over his shoulder, and the front door opened. Four men ran toward him.

He broke into a run, an easy hundred yards separating him from his pursuers.

He passed the small pub a block up from his store, losing them from sight. Then he wondered why he was running when he could simply *travel* somewhere else.

He focused on the bushes behind the store. If he could get back there unseen, they'd never find him. He could hide in the bushes, read his mother's book, and retrieve the knife with his prints on it.

But go where after that? He couldn't go back to his father's house. He couldn't go home.

Maybe the best answer was to go to Frankie's house. Explain to him what was going on and see if Frankie could help. That was probably his only move.

But first, the bushes.

He focused hard, his eyes closed, his panting already calming.

When he opened his eyes, he was standing deep in the bushes. At least twenty yards from the back of the store. He had to pull a branch down to see through its thickness. A section of the brick wall was all he could see.

Good. They won't be able to see me.

He sat down and read.

To my baby Marcus,

I'm so sorry for what you have to go through. You're only eight, but you'll already be a man when you read this.

I'm very proud of you and hope you have found your way. I never meant to hurt you.

But there are some things you must know.

About you.

I want you to imagine a piece of paper—the kind you would have in school. Something eight and a half by eleven. Now, imagine an ant was to walk from one side of the paper to the other. Let's say it was a slow ant that took him ten seconds.

Now fold that paper in half and have the ant go from one end to the other. You'll notice this ant takes one step, and he's already at the other end of the paper because you've folded it.

That's a simple example of what my research team has done with time. We have bent matter and time, so instead of walking from one side of a normal day to the other, we are able to take one step (bending the time version of that school paper) and be at the other end.

Think of time as the sun's rays. Because the sun's rays take eight minutes to travel the millions of miles to get to us, we're feeling the heat and seeing the light of the sun's past.

Without getting too technical, we don't live in a three-dimensional world. We live in a four-dimensional world. There are three dimensions of space and one dimension of time. All we've done is learn how to manipulate that last dimension.

I'm a scientist. I learned, along with my colleagues, how to make my mind into that ant, and time, the paper. Think of it as jumping train tracks—parallel realities. To go back, you just jump tracks because time is linear. Parallel universes allow us to jump tracks.

The difference between fiction and reality is that fiction has to make sense, whereas reality doesn't.

If this isn't making sense, maybe it's because it doesn't have to. I've watched you travel through time, though. Maybe instead of trying to teach you what I did, I'll explain the perils of your gift.

The first problem is you can only go back in time, never forward. Since time hasn't happened yet, there's nowhere in the future to go. You can only go twelve to twenty-four hours maximum when you go back. Only once did I go back two days, but I really had to focus on doing this, and I don't think I could ever do it again.

Because you're out of sync with the fourth dimension when you've traveled, the universe attempts to right itself. As you're brought back, the current time will overlap, and you'll see images like ghosts appear until they solidify. Once they've locked back in, there is a swooshing sound—then you're fully back.

I'm probably describing everything you already know.

This is risky, and I recommend you cease all traveling if you're doing it now or have done it in the past. I'm sorry this has happened, but it's too late for platitudes.

There's one other major problem with traveling, and it concerns blood.

If you are ever back in time somewhere and ...

The handwriting stopped, marred by moisture from something years ago. Marcus flipped the brittle pages one after another until he reached the end of the book.

There was nothing else legible.

"What's the problem with blood, Mom?" he whispered out loud. "Blood as in family or blood as in I can't bleed while traveling or something like that?"

A commotion at the back of the store grew louder. Vehicles pulled up. Car doors opened and closed.

Men argued about something. He heard his name a couple of times.

But most of it was a world away. Even if they trudged through the thick bushes to get to him, he would just disappear.

They didn't worry him anymore.

The problem his mother wrote about worried him.

What did you try to tell me? What problem about blood?

He turned the pages slower, searching between them, around them. At the back of the book, something stuck out of the corner of the inside of the leather-bound cover.

He pinched a finger and thumb on the corner of it and pulled.

It was a photo of a couple sitting at a table having drinks at a café. It looked like a street in Europe from years ago. Older cars, cafés, scooters.

He blinked and looked closer. He was sure the couple was his parents from before he was born. He flipped the picture over. On the back, it said, "*Your father and I are having a drink in Paris. I'm at the table with him in real-time, and I'm waving in the background, wearing the same black outfit, having traveled back to that lunch. I had a tourist take the photo to prove that time travel does work.*"

Marcus flipped the photo back over, and sure enough, a woman, almost identical in size and shape to his mother, wearing the exact same outfit, stood behind his father, her arm suspended in a wave.

He looked up at the clear sky above him, mystified by what he had learned.

Something rustled in the bushes to his right.

What the hell is that?

A dog barked.

Shit!

He closed his eyes, lay back, and focused on his house. Did he want to go home? The cops would be there, too.

Not sure if he should go home, he changed his mind and focused on the Early Onset Neighborly Support Group at the hospital where Samuel Levy worked.

He focused hard and disappeared.

Chapter 14

MARCUS OPENED HIS EYES. He sat on the carpeted floor of the small room they used on Sundays for the support group meetings.

Thankfully, the room was empty. He was alone. His mother's book was still with him as well as the Paris picture.

The door opened.

Samuel Levy entered, flipped on the overhead lights, and jumped, clutching at his chest when he saw Marcus.

"Hey, you scared me," Samuel said. "What are you doing here?"

"I wanted to talk to you about a few things." Marcus got up off the floor and took one of the chairs from a stack that lined the back wall. He pulled a second chair down, carried them across the floor, placed one by Sam, and sat on the other.

"Marcus, I'm working. You know the support group meetings are every two weeks, and it's volunteer, right?"

"Sam, I know all that, but I'm in trouble here, and it's not about Alzheimer's. I need your help, your advice. Could you give me a little of your time? Just five minutes."

"Fine. I'll take my break here, but I must tell the others."

He left and returned a moment later with his lunch bag. From inside the bag, Samuel pulled out two ropes, a needle, and a ball gag.

Marcus tried not to act surprised. "What's that stuff for?"

"It's nothing. Ignore it. You wanted to talk, and I'm willing to listen." Samuel moved his chair closer. "I'm here for you, Marcus. Talk to me."

Marcus told him everything. From the robbery to Katy to the police and what the biker had shown him on the camera in Frankie's office. He couldn't believe it himself, so he explained to Samuel that he would understand if he had trouble wrapping his head around it all.

"So you travel to different locations by your mind alone?" Samuel asked.

"My mother was a scientist. They experimented with time travel when I was in her womb. She didn't know she was pregnant. It affected me somehow. Just like her, I can travel back in time but never into the future."

"Wow, that's quite something." Samuel tapped Marcus's leg with his hand. "Do you have any kind of proof?"

"This." Marcus pulled the picture of the Paris café from his pocket. He extended his hand, passing the picture to Samuel, who examined it.

"Can you explain what I'm looking at?" Samuel asked.

Marcus pointed at his parents. "That's my mom and dad at a café table in Paris. See that woman waving back there?"

"Yeah."

"That's my mother again, after having traveled back so she could be in two places at once. I've already done that today, you know, seen myself, but have no proof of my visits."

Samuel looked skeptical. He touched Marcus's leg again. "That doesn't look like your mom."

"Sure it does. See how she's wearing the same clothes. They're the same body shape and the same hair. One hundred percent that's my mom."

Samuel set the photo down by his lunch bag. "Do you mind if I show this to one of my doctor friends? I would love a second opinion."

"I don't mind, but I want it back before I go see Frankie."

"You're leaving so soon?"

"As soon as we're done talking. I have to go talk to him about the store and Katy. Then I have to go back in time to save Katy."

"Right," Samuel nodded. "You know that here, in this hospital, we're all friends, right, Marcus?"

"Yes. I know we're all friends."

"That's why you came to me, right?"

"Not for that this time," Marcus said, hoping Samuel wouldn't make him take his clothes off again. He was still in pain from the last time. Lately, the things Samuel had done to him weren't part of the support group's agenda. After the meetings, naked, tied up, and being held down, had been torture, but the drugs dulled the senses. Marcus remembered the events in fleeting synapses. Brittle memories that dried up and blew away like dust. When he had lucid moments, he knew what Samuel did to him was wrong, but who would believe Marcus when he couldn't remember anything in detail? All he had were physical scars, a dependency on drugs, and no actual memory of events.

"I came to you," Marcus said. "Because you said you would help me with anything."

"I am your best friend, Marcus," Samuel said in his soothing voice. The voice that brought the sweet release of drugs, then the violation of pain. "You can talk about anything, or we can *do* anything as we're the bestest of friends. Aren't we, little Marcus?"

"We're besties, but I really need your help here. What should I do next? Any advice? I'm really scared, Samuel."

"I think you need to lie down. I think you need to undress and let me massage your problems away."

"No, Samuel, not today. I'm in trouble. I need real help. Not the kind of help that releases tension or causes me more pain. I'm still sore from the last time. Drugs won't help me find Katy."

Samuel raised a finger toward the ceiling. "And you still haven't told anyone about what we do here? Not even Katy?"

Marcus averted his eyes and shook his head.

"I'm willing to offer you real help, Marcus. You wouldn't have come here if you didn't need me or my help. Do you see that needle?"

Marcus looked at the needle. Something inside betrayed him, and yearned for its contents, but he fought the urge.

"There's something extra special in there that'll help you relax. All your problems will go away with that one plunger, and you can travel anywhere you want to. That one needle will set you free. It'll all be over. I'm Samuel, and I'm here to support you, Marcus, with anything you need."

Samuel picked up the needle.

"You came to me for help," Samuel said. "This will help. In a few minutes, nothing will hurt anymore. All your muscles will relax, and you won't remember a thing. Isn't that what you want, Marcus? To forget?"

Fear spun in his belly like it was on a wicked rinse cycle. Something was wrong. What Samuel was proposing had to be against hospital policy. Samuel was risking his job here, and yet he wanted to help. But every time he used the needle to relax, Samuel did things to him, things he could never imagine doing. He was always sore for days after. It had been going on for far too long now, but the needle was desirable. It held a certain lure and generated a yearning inside him.

The needle was too close. If he didn't shove it away, he would grab it and use it.

What is the rope for?

It was time to leave.

Samuel drew closer. His hand rested halfway up Marcus's thigh now. He needed to get to Frankie's to solve everything. Then he could relax, but not until then.

"I'm sorry, Samuel, but I have to go."

Samuel moved fast. The needle was in the air and coming down.

Marcus closed his eyes and filled his consciousness with the image of Frankie's house even as the needle plunged into the meaty part of his thigh.

Chapter 15

THE SUN HAD ROLLED behind clouds when he materialized on the sidewalk a block from Frankie's house. He looked down at his thigh, but the needle had disappeared.

Just in time.

He shuddered at the thought of how close that was. Almost taken by Samuel again. He had to do something about that. Something wasn't quite right. Maybe he would discuss it with his father when this was all done, and Katy was safe again.

He slipped a hand into his pocket. The picture of his parents in Paris was gone.

"Damn, I left it with Samuel," he said out loud.

But Samuel would take care of it. He'll get advice and realize that Marcus was telling the truth.

How could he think Samuel was such a good friend when a part of him begged to stay away from Samuel? Drugs. It had to be the drugs Samuel gave him. Those wonderful injections. At any other time, Marcus might have stayed. But Katy needed him.

He had resisted, and at least now he could move on and deal with the matters at hand without trying to keep the Paris picture safe.

His boss, Frankie, lived in a more expensive area of Brampton. The houses were bigger, with greener lawns than Marcus was used to. The vehicles parked in front of most of the homes cost fifty-thousand dollars or higher. Marcus hadn't heard of some of the names, but he knew they cost heavy dough. Saab, Maserati, Alfa Romeo, Lexus, Lotus.

He walked slowly, taking everything in. There had never been a time in his life when he had this much to digest. Katy was dead. He still couldn't believe it. He had nothing to do with it directly, but the police were hunting him. And all because of Frankie and his biker friends.

His mother's death had been his fault. That was one way to look at it. The grief almost crippled him. He walked with a limp, his hands in his pockets, hoping that a visit with Frankie was the right move because it was one of the last moves.

Maybe he would explain everything to the cops. Maybe he could tell the bikers to go away. Or better yet, they can explain to the cops what they had done, but he realized that probably wouldn't happen.

Most of all, he needed to look Frankie in the eyes and ask what his problem was. They had worked together for two years. How could it all come to this? How could he not have been more truthful?

Then Marcus would travel back in time a few days and fix everything. His mother's book said he could only travel back one day, but he would find a way to do it. He had to. Katy depended on him to figure it out.

He would travel back to Friday, before the weekend, when he spent the day at the store working.

That would give him time to be with Katy and convince himself to quit The Act Of Love so none of the past twenty-four hours would ever exist.

He stopped at Frankie's steps and looked up at the house. It would do him no good to be taken by the bikers again. He had to be sure they weren't here.

Nothing moved in the windows. The house's exterior was the exact opposite of his father's house. Frankie had the lawn cut and the bushes trimmed, and none of the paint was chipped. Everything looked immaculate. Even the windows looked freshly cleaned. Maybe keeping up his house had more to do with the neighborhood than Frankie himself. He had always been one to fit in.

Frankie's Camaro was in the driveway, which normally meant he was home, but he wasn't supposed to be in the store until tomorrow, so Marcus couldn't be sure.

The only way to find out was to knock.

The sidewalk remained empty. Not even one car passed by.

He walked up the small concrete stones toward the front door when a realization hit him. He was a timekeeper, a keeper of time. He was supposed to travel and then travel back to the current time, to where he had originally left. But ever since the interrogation room where the detectives had him cuffed to a table, he had continually traveled, not once going back to where he was last or the original spot. Nothing seemed to be pulling him back, either. Maybe that's what his mother tried to warn him about. Being locked in the past by traveling too many times backward. Or maybe that was the solution to going back four days. Just keep traveling back to twelve hours before, then repeat.

He rapped on the door with the lion head knocker.

A timekeeper. I like that.

He knocked again. Footsteps approached, and the small white curtain slid back to the left of the door.

Frankie peeked out at him, his eyes ragged, almost as bloodshot as a bare-knuckle boxer's hands.

What happened to him?

The lock clicked, but the door didn't open.

"Can I come in?" Marcus asked through the closed door.

A muffled *yes* filtered through.

Marcus stepped inside, fully alert. In that second, he wondered if the bikers had gotten to Frankie and were waiting to jump him from behind the door.

He kept the door open wide, holding the knob.

"What's going on, Frankie?"

His boss hadn't looked at him as he moved slowly down the hall toward the kitchen.

"Just come on in. We'll talk. Get it over with."

Marcus looked behind the door. He checked the meet-and-greet room to the right and glanced up the stairs off the central foyer before shutting the door. He listened for any noises or telltale signs of others in the house but heard nothing.

"Who else is here?" he shouted.

"You just missed them," Frankie said from the kitchen.

"Missed who?"

"Come to the kitchen. I got coffee."

Two years of knowing Frankie motivated Marcus to walk the tile floor to Frankie's kitchen. Even with that, the hair on the back of his neck stood up straight.

He leaned on the doorframe at the kitchen door, still not ready to commit to being in the same room with the man he wasn't sure he knew anymore.

Frankie turned to him, and for the first time, he saw the effect of his age on his face. A sense of pity and empathy filled Marcus. How could Frankie have chosen this life, whatever it was, when he had a successful business, money, and whatever else he wanted?

"You don't look so good," Marcus said.

"Neither do you." Frankie pointed at Marcus's cheek and rolled his finger in a circle. "What happened?"

"Long story. But I have a few questions for you first."

Frankie nodded, stepped away from the coffee maker, and picked up a pack of cigarettes on the table.

"Want one?" he asked, holding the pack in the air.

"I don't smoke, and you know that. When are you going to quit?"

Frankie shrugged and looked at the pack in his hand. "When are you gonna start?" He flipped one out, stuck it between his lips, and tossed the pack on the table. "You think I can remember who smokes and who doesn't?" He patted his pockets in search of a light, saw the matches on the counter, and headed that way.

"We have trouble at the store," Marcus said.

"I know."

"How? Weren't you *busy* this weekend?"

Frankie struck a match, held it to the tip of the cigarette, and stared through the smoke at Marcus. That stare made him feel like he was sitting in the principal's office in high school. This was his boss. When he stared like that, Marcus was about to be cussed out.

"Why did you do it?" Frankie asked.

"Do what?"

Frankie grabbed two mugs, poured coffee, and set them on the table. The tension felt thick enough to gel the coffee into sludge.

"Cream?" Frankie asked. "Sugar?"

"Black."

Frankie sat in front of his cup and puffed hard on his cigarette. After a moment of silence, Marcus moved to the table and sat down.

"The police just left half an hour ago," Frankie started.

"What did they want?"

"You."

Marcus put on a surprised look. "Me? Did they say what for?"

"Some shit about you robbing the store."

Marcus wrapped his hands around the coffee mug so Frankie wouldn't see them shaking. "They've got some nerve."

"Did you rob the store, or didn't you?"

"Frankie, come on," Marcus said, sitting ramrod straight. "You think I'd steal from *you*?"

Frankie's bloodshot eyes met his gaze, locked for a moment, then dropped to stare at his cup as he drank from it.

"Marcus, I can't have the cops around my house."

"I understand—"

Frankie smashed the table with his fist, sloshing Marcus's coffee over the rim of his cup and making Marcus physically jump in his seat.

"No, you don't!" he shouted. "Nothing will take me down after all I've been through and how close I am to going clean. I've almost bought my way out."

"Okay, okay," Marcus said, his hands up. "Take it easy."

"Don't tell me to take it easy in my house. Do you know how hard it is to drive to that jail cell every Friday night? I need all day Monday to get it out of my blood. This was my last weekend, and this is the weekend my store is hit. I can't have any of this blowback on me."

"Nothing will."

"How can you be so certain? Sounds like you know more than you're letting on." He jammed the half-smoked cigarette into the dirty ashtray on the table and looked back at Marcus. "Where's Katy?"

"What?"

"The police said they were worried about her. Know anything about that?"

Marcus shook his head back and forth, not trusting his voice at that moment.

Remember to stay calm. Disappear if this gets too intense.

"How are we going to make this right?" Frankie asked. "I have to make this right."

"What are you talking about? Make what right? With who?"

"This goes back a long way," Frankie said. He drank more from his cup. "I ran with the wrong people years ago."

"To get out, to stop doing what I was doing, I had to pay my way out. That meant running the store for them. I had to do what they asked. Even this house is theirs."

"Who are they?"

"One more month, and I was out," Frankie said as if he didn't hear Marcus's question. "New managers were coming in. New blood. New recruits." He shook his head and grabbed for the cigarette pack. "But then you had to do what you did."

"What are you talking about? All I did—"

"Shut up!" Frankie yelled. "You talk when I'm fucking well done."

Marcus wanted to leave. The only thing rooting him to the chair was the need to know more of what Frankie was about to say.

After lighting another cigarette, puffing hard on it twice, and blowing the smoke directly over his head, Frankie looked through the glass doors that led onto the large back deck. Marcus followed his gaze and stared at the barbecue Frankie had used earlier in the summer when he had him and Katy over for dinner.

"The police showed me the store's camera feed," Frankie said. "They explained what they think you did and what they thought of the blood at your house. They told me Katy's missing and fear the worst." He looked at Marcus. "When the consortium saw what you did and sent a couple of guys to fix the problem, you attacked them and ran away. Do you know how this looks to me? For you? Are you aware of what they do to people like you? What they will do to anyone you love?"

Marcus's lower lip quivered. He couldn't stop it. The coffee that had spilled from his cup framed the bottom in an odd shape. He stared at it, trying to get his roiling stomach under control. Whatever happened today, whatever happened tomorrow, he was sure he would be in a lot of trouble and not just the police kind. He would never have believed how far his life had unraveled in such a short time or that it was even possible.

I just have to travel back four days. That'll fix everything.

"They think you work for me," Frankie said. "They think I did this. But I tried to convince them otherwise. And do you know what the problem with that is?"

Marcus shook his head.

"The problem with that is all this comes down on you." Frankie pointed at him with his cigarette. "That's the kind of weight good men like you never recover from, Marcus."

"What do we do, then?"

"*We* don't do anything. *You* have to make this right." Frankie pointed at Marcus with his cigarette hand.

"How do I do that?"

"Meet with them. Tell them the truth."

"What'll they do to me?"

"I have no idea, but it won't be pretty. Maybe you'll have to *buy* your way out of their grasp as well."

Marcus looked down at the table. It had only been a little money. How could he lose his Katy and have to make it right with these people? It didn't make sense to him, but it started to make him angry.

"You know what," Marcus said through clenched teeth. "I think they have to make it right with me."

Frankie leaned back and raised his eyebrows. His hands rested on the edge of the table as white smoke circled his head. "How do you figure that?"

"Katy."

"They claim you did that. All they did was take her body to dispose of it as they've got ways of disposing of bodies that you don't."

His heart doubled in speed. His stomach clenched as he tried to find his voice.

"What did … you say?" He looked down, breathed in and out, and then stared back at Frankie, anger growing inside him like he'd never felt before. If he wanted to, he could destroy the table, break Frankie in half, and take on a dozen bikers in this state of rage before he calmed down to eat a sandwich.

"I said they helped you."

"Where's Katy?" Marcus asked.

"If they didn't deal with her body, it would leave a trail back to them. Neighbors saw the black van. A dead woman creates too many questions." Frankie butted his smoke out in the ashtray. "Are you seeing the kind of people you're dealing with yet? They're ruthless, cunning, strong, and smart. They don't let people like you or me fuck with them."

"None of that matters now. Where are they? We'll see who fucks with who."

Frankie leaned back and chuckled. "You're such a child. You think your little temper tantrum will hurt them? That kind of anger clouds your judgment. You can't think, you can't fight, you won't survive."

"Where are they?" Marcus shouted louder than he intended.

Frankie pushed his chair back and stood.

"First, you and I have to make it right."

"What does that mean?" Marcus asked.

Frankie slid the large square ring off his right hand's middle finger. He pulled his sleeve up, then yanked the other one up past the elbow.

Marcus stayed seated. "What are you doing, Frankie? This isn't necessary."

Maybe Frankie was right. The anger from a moment ago dissipated fast in the face of fear. He didn't want to fight Frankie. That was juvenile and accomplished nothing.

Marcus looked away. Maybe Frankie would wait. Maybe they would talk more. Solve this another way.

"Marcus, look at me. We have to make this right."

"This doesn't make anything right."

"Look at me."

Marcus started to cry.

I'm twenty-eight years old, and I'm crying like a baby. Yeah, maybe because you haven't had a fight since grade six.

"I'm not going to fight you."

"Stand up and man up, or I'll drive my fist into the back of your skull."

The anger resurfaced. How could Frankie talk to him this way, treat him like this? After all Marcus had done for him, this wasn't right. It didn't make anything right.

He realized that maybe he deserved it. For what happened to Katy, maybe he deserved a beat down.

Or should he just disappear?

Before he could think about it again, Marcus stood and faced Frankie.

The fist came so fast that all he saw was a blur. It hit the stitches dead on, drove the bandage into his face, and knocked him clean off his feet. A glimpse of light flashed across his vision, and the room wavered around him.

Am I traveling back to the interrogation room?

He sprawled out on the floor of Frankie's kitchen and opened his eyes. He moaned, not wanting to move. Even as he heard more footsteps approaching, he didn't move. The last thing he wanted was to get up and get hit again.

"Good job," a man said. "We believe you now."

Who the hell is that?

"We'll take him from here. You're cleared."

Are the cops here?

He looked at the newcomer. The biker from his house this morning. The one with the gun.

"No," Marcus mumbled. "Not you."

The biker smiled. "Sorry to disappoint."

Two men dressed in black leather jackets entered the kitchen.

"Take him out the back to the van. Make sure he can't squeal. And hold tight. This one's slippery."

Blood dripped into his ear from the cut on his face. He saw Frankie looking down at him, his face unreadable. He realized he had no idea who Frankie was. The man was a stranger to him now. Actually, more than that. An enemy.

He closed his eyes and focused on his father's quiet backyard. He channeled the pain, the hurt, the anger, and the fear. He allowed it all to funnel down into his soul and struggled hard to ensure he would travel to his father's yard.

Rough hands yanked his mouth open and jammed a piece of cloth in so hard he thought his jaw would break in the open position.

He screamed through the cloth and tried to see what they were doing.

He hadn't traveled anywhere. He'd only needed an extra second or two. The bikers in Frankie's kitchen lifted him to his feet.

They manhandled him so roughly he could almost feel the bruises forming on his arms as they touched him.

The head biker was talking to Frankie, saying something about absolving him from the crime at the store. Nothing would fall back on him. Letting them listen in from the other room had just cleared him of any wrongdoing. Some boss man was going to be called. Everything was all good now.

Then the biker pulled out a gun.

Before the other two bikers turned Marcus away, the biker who had chased Marcus that morning with a gun in his hand placed the weapon on Frankie's forehead and pulled the trigger.

Frankie fell in slow motion, his face a mask of terror and surprise.

Marcus's body revolted, and he vomited into his mouth, the gag pooling it at his throat. His stomach contracted again, jamming its contents in his throat. As he choked on his own vomit, he wondered if he would see Katy on the other side or if he was going to Hell.

One of the bikers ripped the cloth out of his mouth. The load in his mouth spewed out with it. He gagged, coughed, and threw up again.

"Gross," one yelled.

"You fucking ass," the other one said. "I got some on my arm."

Marcus fell to the floor, his head sideways, coughing until his throat cleared. He looked across the kitchen floor at Frankie's open dead eyes while brown saliva dribbled from the corner of his mouth. His half-finished cigarette billowed white smoke off the floor, where it fell in front of Frankie's gaping mouth.

Then they were turning him over. They jammed another cloth into his mouth and lifted him to his feet.

"Bring him to me," the shooter said.

They dragged him to the biker who stood over Frankie's body.

Marcus's right arm was yanked up, and his fingers splayed open. The biker placed the gun in it, wrapped Marcus's fingers around the handle, pressed them firmly, and then released him.

The biker nodded, and the men dragged him out of Frankie's kitchen, down the back walkway, which was concealed by eight-foot hedges on either side, and into the yawning back doors of a black van.

To him, the doors represented the beast's open mouth that would consume him. His life was over. Katy was dead, and now Frankie was gone. There was no way to recover from this carnage.

The worst part was that he figured out what his mother's warning was when she said in the book his dad gave him … *and it concerns blood.*

He couldn't time travel while bleeding. Blood was his essence; if it leaked, he couldn't transport it anywhere.

When Frankie had hit him, he'd reopened the knife wound on his face. That was the only reason he could come up with for not traveling away in the time it had taken to close his eyes and focus.

He was stuck with these homicidal maniacs until he stopped bleeding.

If they would let him stop bleeding.

Chapter 16

Detective Bruce Green stood in the bushes at the back of The Act Of Love, staring down at the imprint of a man's body on the weeds, and shook his head.

"How the hell do you keep evading us?" he asked the air.

His cell phone rang.

"Green here."

"Shots fired at a residence in Brampton," Steve Walton said. Green and Walton had gone to high school together in Oshawa, partied a lot, and stayed in touch, helping each other out when they could. He worked for Peel regional police as a senior dispatcher and was a real asset for Green at times. He got to review and see almost all the incoming calls. "Local units responding. Just thought you should know."

"What would that have to do with me?" Green asked. "By the way, nice to hear from you."

"You too. You're working the Marcus Johnson case, right?"

"Yeah."

"It's the personal residence of the owner of The Act Of Love, Frankie Cardelli. A black van was spotted leaving the area."

"Got an address?"

Walton gave it to him.

"Thanks. I owe you one."

"Beer. I need beer."

"This weekend. On me."

"It's been a few months. Make it happen."

"Done."

Green hung up.

"Smith, we have to go."

"Where?" Detective Smith burst through a row of bushes and stepped up to Green's side.

"Shots fired at Frankie's house."

"What? Really? You think Marcus is there?"

Green nodded.

"Then who was here?"

"No idea. Maybe nobody. A ghost. Doesn't matter. Brampton locals are going to trample all over our case. We have to get up there, pronto."

"Then let's go. Follow me."

Smith turned and pushed through the foliage.

Green stayed close.

Chapter 17

They didn't blindfold him. The whole way to their warehouse north of the city, they didn't care that he saw where they were going. He could easily reveal the route to the cops at a later date. Having no blindfold meant this was a one-way trip.

He hung his head.

Fate had a funny way of revealing itself. He had never met the kind of men who could kill another human being as easily as swatting a fly. Having seen their faces, watched them kill Frankie in his kitchen, and still not have a blindfold on as they drove him to wherever it was they were going, Marcus knew this was the end. His life, his story, his struggle. An end. Just like Katy and Frankie. A morbid finish orchestrated by an evil he couldn't understand.

Maybe he deserved it. The ball started rolling because of him. The theft, the violence, the knife with his prints, everything because of him.

His comeuppance. His restitution. The consequence for his deeds.

But was death the answer? Is that the consequence of a robbery and an accident? Or did he deserve to die?

A morsel of hope stirred inside him. He didn't deserve to die. He hadn't intended to hurt Katy. He had nothing to do with Frankie's death. If anyone deserved to die, it was the bikers who had perpetrated everything from the start. They were the ones committing crimes, hurting people, killing people.

He never thought a biker gang would kill him because he had wanted a little of what he felt was his. The entitlement curse. The belief that some of what Frankie had built up had to be Marcus's since he was the one who had worked more than forty hours a week for two years building up the business.

But unbeknownst to Marcus, he had stepped on toes he couldn't see. It wasn't his fault. He had no idea who was involved and why. Had he known any of it, he never would've stolen the money. In fact, he would've quit that job months ago, if not last year. Let some other clerk deal with the bullshit.

It wasn't fair that he paid for this with his life. He had to fight. He had to find a way out of their grip.

He decided to wait and watch for an opening. Be attentive. Listen. When he stopped bleeding, he would simply eject himself. They would be mystified about how he escaped and begin looking for him.

But this time, he would travel back through time to the police station. He would wait and let time catch up. That meant, eventually, he would be pulled back to that interrogation room, the cuffs reapplied. The two detectives would enter the room as if he hadn't even left, and he would tell them the whole sordid tale, even describing the way to get to the biker's clubhouse near Orangeville.

He would win. Because of the power his mother bestowed on him, he could win. He would do it for Katy. And even though he owed Frankie nothing, he would do it for Frankie too because it wasn't right that he got shot in his kitchen like that.

Unless I could do what my mother couldn't and travel back four days to Friday ...

The van stopped in front of an old farmhouse with a barn attached at the back. The smell of cow manure hit him as soon as the van's door slid open.

The rag was still jammed in his mouth, his tongue pushed back and immovable.

He waited until they told him to move. The stress on the stitches in his cheek ached. Because his mouth was jammed open wide with the rag in it, the skin on his cheeks was being stretched. Some of the stitches had popped, and the rest felt like they were being pulled out slowly. It would be a blessing to have the rag taken from his mouth.

The two men hopped out the side and gestured for him to follow.

He crawled to the edge gingerly, then swung his legs over the rim of the van.

The biker who shot Frankie walked up and stood in front of Marcus.

"We brought you to see Katy."

Marcus arched an eyebrow in hope. Maybe she was still alive. Or did he mean they were going to bury him with her?

"She's in the barn. You get to spend the night together." He stepped away, then looked back to address his men. "Bring him to the barn."

Both men grabbed his arms and guided him toward the barn, following their leader.

The barn doors were large and reminded him of doors in books from his childhood. Pieces of wood were nailed in the shape of the letter Z on each door for support.

The biker lifted off a three-foot piece of wood held by metal clasps and set it on the dirt to the right. Then he pulled on the door and opened it slowly.

The smell of putrefaction caused him to rear back in horror. A cow or a couple of pigs. Something was decaying. The smell was unmistakable.

The leader turned around, his thumb and finger holding his nose closed.

In a nasal voice, he said, "Enjoy the accommodations, asshole."

Then he hit him.

The biker's fist was as fast as Frankie's, a blur, a hammer breaking his cheek's flesh even further. The pain was brutal, stunning, and scary. Because of the new hit, more blood would flow. The wound was reopened. He would have no chance to travel out of here for hours. Whatever they had planned for him was coming no matter what, and there was nothing he could do about it. That realization hurt more than the pain in his face.

His knees weakened, but he wasn't about to fall as the men on each side held him firmly.

The biker examined his hand and saw blood on his knuckles. He pulled the rag from Marcus's mouth. It caused another gasp from him as the flesh of his cheek dropped back in place after being jammed open for so long.

The biker used a clean part of the rag to wipe the blood off his knuckles.

"Are you going to be any trouble?" he asked.

Defeated, Marcus shook his head, afraid to move his mouth to talk.

"Good. Boys, take him inside to get reacquainted with his woman."

The men dragged him inside the dark barn to a horror Marcus couldn't endure.

Marcus's mind slipped. Then it was completely lost.

Chapter 18

"WHAT HAVE WE GOT here?" Detective Green asked.

He wore little booties on his shoes, a cap for his hair, and gloves. Detective Spinoza, who was strict about crime-scene contamination, was jotting notes on a pad. She stopped writing, lowered her glasses to the tip of her nose, and looked directly at Green.

"How did you hear about my case all the way downtown?" she asked.

"I have an arrest warrant for Marcus Johnson, our main man in the disappearance and suspected murder of Katy Webster. He's also wanted for the robbery of The Act of Love, the adult store he worked at, which is owned by the man with a bullet in his forehead on this kitchen floor." He pointed at the corpse in front of him. "This was Marcus Johnson's boss at the adult store. That's how I heard about this. Active case."

Men in white coveralls walked around him, milling about the area. One was on his hands and knees, examining every inch of the kitchen floor. Another was dusting the cups on the kitchen table. The gun used had been printed and bagged.

Every law enforcement official in the Golden Horseshoe

surrounding Lake Ontario on the western side, from Toronto to Niagara Falls, knew how efficient Spinoza was and how fast she worked. She had one of the best conviction rates this side of the earth, and the fact that Green was standing in the kitchen where the murder occurred told him she was willing to share information. But he knew she would make him crawl for it.

"You think this is Marcus's doing?" she asked.

"No idea who did this."

"Then why are you here?"

She walked past him to the front door and down the steps. She stopped on the front lawn and pulled out her cell phone.

Green followed her out. At the front door, he ripped off the booties wrapped around his black dress shoes, tore off the cap covering his hair, and slipped out of the gloves they had supplied him with.

He nodded at the officer handling the murder log, who clocked him out of the house at the right time, keeping track of everyone who entered and exited the crime scene.

The sun had started its descent. Green stood on the lawn under its summer power and sweated, waiting for Spinoza to get off the phone. She spoke part English, part Spanish. He couldn't tell if it was a personal call or not, but he could tell she was fucking with him, making him wait and sweat.

His partner, Smith, sat in their air-conditioned cruiser, watching the action of the crime-scene team as they came and went. Spinoza had limited access to her crime scenes, so only one could come in. It was a no-brainer that Green would be the one. He respected Spinoza more than Smith did, which had cost him two years ago on another case. Spinoza had a case almost thrown out because of Smith's actions. Her case ended up getting plea bargained, and her perp got out in six months instead of ten years.

Spinoza hated Smith because of that and, by extension, didn't like

Green much either.

They had Marcus in custody that morning, lost him because of a defective interrogation door—news like that spread like wildfire throughout every police department in Ontario—and now Marcus's boss had been shot. The possible, if not probable, shooter was Marcus Johnson, which might be enough for them to lose their badges.

That left them with no option but to chase this case to its conclusion. The alternative was to walk away and face possible charges.

Spinoza closed her phone. "Was there something else?"

Green faced her, squinting into the sun. He raised a hand to shield his eyes.

"Any witnesses?" he asked. "Neighbors see anything? Prints on the weapon? A suicide note left behind? Anything that points to Marcus?" He waited a moment. Then added, "Or a biker gang?"

A stone monument moved more often than her face. But at the mention of a biker gang, a muscle twitched under her right eye. He'd hit a nerve.

Good. Bitch.

"I've got officers canvassing the neighborhood. My crime-scene guys are dusting inside, and no notes have been found. Anything else?" The last two words came out with spittle.

Marcus was his case. She would have to contact him if she found something tied to Marcus. Shoe on the other foot stuff.

"No. Nothing else."

He turned away and started for his car. She called his name. He took three more deliberate steps, slowed, then stopped.

Without turning around so as not to reveal his smile, he said, "What is it?"

"Biker gang?" she asked.

He straightened his mouth and turned around. Their eyes met. "I have witnesses who I talked to myself that swear members of the Spawns Motorcycle Club were at Marcus's house this morning. Frankie had known ties to biker gangs in years past." He shrugged. "Probably nothing. But if they're settling a score and Marcus happened to get in the way …"

He let the ending trail off. Nothing was left to be said. If his hypothesis were correct, then an entire phalanx of possible avenues would have to be exhausted before they figured everything out. This case could take months, if not longer. Add to that Marcus's unique ability to escape their clutches, and a lot of good men would be up before the disciplinary hearings office soon enough.

Spinoza looked at her phone and then shoved it into her jacket pocket. Her stare was as cold as her face and as solid as marble.

Green waited.

"I'll call you," she said, "if we find something I think might help."

Green walked away without a word.

"Wait," she called.

He stopped.

"You'll do the same?"

He nodded, twisted around, and blocked the sun with his hand.

By the side of the house, bushes shook. His eyes moved that way.

Green stared at the bushes so long he detected Spinoza turning in his peripheral vision.

They shook again. A hand from inside the foliage lifted up and clamped onto the window sill. Then, whoever was hiding in the bush, pulled himself up to look in the kitchen window.

Marcus Johnson.

Are you fucking kidding me?

It had to be Marcus, but with the sun in his eyes, he couldn't be sure.

Green ran past Spinoza, headed for the bushes.

Chapter 19

Katy's body was in the other corner of the stall.

Despair filled Marcus's soul. He rolled into a ball on the dirty ground of the barn. The straw had been removed. Steel bars had been welded together in place of the stall door to create a crude jail cell. He had tried the bars and the barred window, but nothing budged.

There was no way out.

Except one.

But he couldn't travel until he stopped bleeding. The last time he checked, his face still leaked, and his bandage was ruined. Only the bottom part of the bandage still clung to his skin.

Sunlight invaded the crude cell through a small window just above his head. There was plenty of light to see her discolored face, the dried blood where something had hit her in the side of the head.

"I'm so sorry—" Marcus whispered.

He gagged, choked on mucus, and swallowed. Then the tears came, long and hard, body-wracking sobs, violent grief. He curled up and rode the wave of grief until it subsided to something more manageable.

He could do it. He could fix this.

Why am I letting them win?

He wiped at his tears, his hand coming away bloody.

The bleeding had to stop, or he couldn't fix anything. His pockets held nothing. He didn't even have his wallet. Dabbing his shirt against his cheek wouldn't work as the stitches had weakened and the wound reopened. He needed something else, something stronger.

Then he remembered what Katy had said to him that morning in the bathroom before the madness had started.

"I've got gauze and extra bandages in my pocket here."

He should have gone down for a cup of tea with her. She had just shown him the plaque on the wall that represented their relationship.

It all started because two people fell in love.

How could he face her? She had died because of what he had done. The guilt weighed too much on his soul. The despair dragged him down as if Lucifer himself watched from the loft in the barn, his black wings gently stroking the air, a smile playing across his fiery lips as he grinned and chuckled at the banality of it all.

Only Lucifer watched over Marcus's lost soul now. Marcus's mother gave him life and took her own because of him. Katy died as a result of his thievery. Would the bikers have killed Frankie if none of this had happened? How many people had to die for him? How many more would deposit their souls in Satan's bank account for Marcus, where the withdrawal was eternal damnation?

The choices left for him were simple.

Be killed by homicidal bikers and burn in hell for the deaths he'd caused and the choices he'd made, or fix this by traveling back to when Katy was still alive and hoping to hell that God would see fit to forgive him and forget.

He rolled onto his back. Then rolled again and repeated this process until he was lying beside the corpse of his woman. The smell of rotting death intensified beside her, but he had no choice. In order to erase this version of her, he had to go into her pocket.

Slowly, he moved his hand sideways until it touched hers. Rigor mortis had already set in; her fingers crimped up. It wouldn't be long before they loosened and settled back until decay took the flesh and fed an unseen bacteria. He only wished they could trade spots. Death, at this point, erased the pain for him.

He laced his fingers inside hers and tightened his grip. The flesh on Katy's fingers didn't respond like normal. Instead, it kind of melted into his grasp. It was like he had closed his eyes and imagined squeezing a slab of liver at the butcher shop.

He held her hand nonetheless. It was Katy, and this was only a pit stop. Within hours, they would be back in bed together, and this would be nothing more than a nightmare. He would wake, look upon her still form, and touch her flesh, and it would rebound like normal. The giver of life was nothing more than the ability to manipulate time. God could do it, and now he had bestowed that ability upon Marcus.

"Don't worry, honey bunny. I'm coming for you. Just give me a little time."

With his other hand, he brought it around and tried to slip it into her pants pocket. In Katy's hip area, what felt like a gas buildup under the skin gave way. His hand dipped lower than normal. His stomach reminded him to hurry, or it would seize again and send the product of its contractions northward.

The bandage and gauze were right where she had put them that morning. Between his thumb and forefinger, he gripped it tight, so he didn't fumble and have to go inside for a second time. He pulled slowly. Both items withdrew from her jeans without protest.

He let go of her hand and rolled away. Even though the air smelled the same wherever he was in the stall, he took a deep breath when he reached the far side. It just tasted better this far from death.

He tore off the bandage from his face and tossed it on the ground.

After unwrapping the new bandage, he dabbed at the wound with the gauze and bandaged it back up again as best he could without a mirror.

Then he sat in the corner of the stall. No more lying down. He needed his face to remain higher than his heart to make it even harder to bleed from the wound.

Clot, baby, clot.

While he waited in the corner of the stall, he thought of Katy and the wonderful times they had shared together. He focused on Friday morning, waking, having the lemon potatoes from last night's dinner as hash browns, and eggs, sunny side up so they could dip the potatoes into the yolks. He could almost taste it. The conversation. Katy's smile. Her smell.

It was a form of meditation to travel somewhere else. All he had to do was focus hard enough, and he'd leave this wretched place.

Two male voices drew near. One laughed.

He opened his eyes. He was still in the barn. Katy still decayed twelve feet away.

A door clicked somewhere in the barn.

Someone was coming.

"Are you still here?" the biker shouted.

Marcus closed his eyes and focused harder. He could hear Katy's Friday morning voice. He could smell the cooking.

"I've brought someone to see you," the biker intruded. "Someone you've known for years. He wants to have a word with you. Or his way with you." The biker laughed. "Marcus Johnson, let me present to you your dear friend, Samuel Levy, from your support group at the hospital. He's even brought his medical kit so you can have a nice ride with him."

It pulled Marcus out of his trance and made him think of his boss. Frankie would've stuck up for him. The Frankie he knew would've saved him from assholes like the biker. They had been pals, friends. It saddened him that Frankie had died the way he did.

A breeze ruffled his hair.

Marcus opened his eyes and looked around. He was in the bushes beside Frankie's house, just under the kitchen window.

But did he travel back far enough in time to save Frankie?

***

By the time Green got to the bushes, whoever had been hiding in them had ducked back down. The sun's rays blocked most of his direct line of sight, but the bushes were still moving as he spread them apart.

Detective Green saw nothing but stems, tiny leaves, and dirt at the base of the bushes.

Spinoza came up behind him. "Do you mind telling me what you think you're doing?"

He let the bushes fall back in place. After a deep breath to calm his racing heart from the run, he turned around to address her.

"I thought I saw something."

"Something? Or someone?"

"Did you see him, too?"

She crossed her arms and took an aggressive posture. Three of the officers working the scene moved closer to listen in.

"There's no one in that bush, Detective Green. Would you agree?"

"Obviously." His patience for her overbearing, mothering attitude was running thin. "It's simple, Spinoza. I thought I saw something. Here I am. I looked. It's nothing."

"Are you doing okay? House? Family? Wife?"

"Thanks for your concern." He walked past her. "I feel so much better already. Knowing you care so much." After a few more paces, he called over his shoulder. "Call me when you want to share information."

Smith had gotten out of the car when he saw Green run across Frankie's front lawn.

"Everything okay?" Smith asked, leaning on the open car door.

"Yeah, it's nothing."

"What happened?"

"Just visions of Marcus coming and going again."

"Maybe there's something to that," Smith said, his face scrunched up against the setting sun.

"Get in the car, Smith. We're outta here."

"10-4."

Smith dropped back in the car.

Green paused at his door and looked at the house. Spinoza had remained by the bushes, her arms crossed. She had watched him walk the length of the lawn.

He nodded at her.

She didn't move. Stone again.

"Bitch," he muttered and climbed into the car.

"Where to next?" Smith asked.

"To talk to any known associates of Marcus. Do we have a lead on any of his friends?"

"His father told us about that Alzheimer's support group he goes to bi-weekly up at the hospital. Maybe someone there might have something useful."

"What was the name of that group again?" Green started the car and pulled away from the curb.

"The E.O.N.S."

"What's it stand for?"

"The Early Onset Neighborly Support group."

"Great. Why isn't it the E.O.N.S.G.," he said, emphasizing the G sound.

"Maybe they forgot the word Group was in their title."

Green looked over at his partner. Smith shrugged.

"That's not funny," Green said. "These people are afflicted with a disease that virtually erases their memory at an early age, and you're making jokes at their expense. Maybe they forgot …"

"Fine. Forget I said it, then."

Green grunted. "Stop already."

***

At the window, Marcus saw Frankie still dead on his kitchen floor, but the room was filled with at least a dozen men dressed in white bodysuits.

He hadn't traveled back far enough. To his left, someone was running across the lawn at him.

Marcus dropped below the cover of the bushes and placed a hand at each temple. He breathed in the scent of the bushes and focused on staying right where he was, five hours before the current time.

He thought about arriving on the sidewalk, one city block from Frankie's house, and how that felt. Where the sun was, how the air felt, the temperature, and the direction the breeze flowed.

Then he focused harder, believing he was there.

Someone reached the bushes and yanked on them at the exact second he slipped back in time.

It almost felt like he made the man who had arrived at the bushes time travel away from him because nothing had changed for Marcus. He still sat in the bushes, surrounded by prickly stems, the wet dirt soaking into his ass. But the man had disappeared.

It had gotten easier. He was mastering his ability. He assumed his mother had mastered her ability over time and made it work for her, too. That was all he needed to do. Make this work for him instead of the other way around.

He got up slowly and checked his surroundings. He couldn't barge in because his earlier self might be inside, already talking to Frankie.

At the kitchen window, he cupped his hands and looked inside. Frankie was alone at the kitchen table, smoking.

Marcus eased out of the bushes and walked toward the front of the house to see if his earlier self had arrived yet.

The sidewalk was empty.

This gave him time to talk to Frankie and save him before he or the bikers showed up.

Unless the bikers were already here. If he entered Frankie's house, they would come out of hiding, kill Frankie and take him again. Everything would be for naught if he let that happen.

There had to be another way.

But what would happen if he stopped himself from being taken by the bikers? Would he see Katy's body? Would he use the bandage he found in her pocket? Would he even exist as a time traveler in this incarnation, or would he be zapped somewhere else?

The word paradox came to him. What exactly was that, and how would it affect him?

Shit. Now what?

He had to save Frankie's life. That was first and foremost. Then he could go back and save Katy.

That would stop the nightmare from ever happening. He had to stop confusing himself.

A vehicle on the street broke him from his thoughts. Marcus crept around the side of the house to look. A black van crawled along the quiet suburban road and pulled into the back of Frankie's house. The two bikers got out.

It was too late to talk to Frankie alone.

He waited until they entered the house, where they met with

Frankie in the kitchen. Through the window, he heard them arguing about money. His name came up a couple of times.

He chanced a peek but then dropped from sight when he saw one of the bikers look his way.

He waited a little longer. When he couldn't hear their voices anymore, he chanced another look.

The kitchen was empty. Frankie's cigarette sat in the ashtray on the table, a line of white smoke rising from the tip.

Where did they go?

He dropped below the cover of the bushes again, his stomach on full nervous duty.

What now?

Maybe he should try to focus on Friday. Maybe he should just get back to the beginning, stop the robbery, save Katy, and then Frankie wouldn't even come into this. Actually, Frankie had been in a weekend jail, so nothing would happen to anyone if he could travel back to Friday.

But what would happen when the current time caught up to him? What would the world look like if he changed the past?

There was no other choice, though. He had to go back for Katy.

He held his temples and began the meditation for Friday. The meditation of escape.

Hands grabbed his wrists before he could dig deep into his mental attempt at traveling.

He was lifted from the bushes and thrown down onto the grass.

"What do we have here?" the head biker said. "Always escaping us. Always able to get away." He kicked Marcus in the side. "Well, not anymore."

Marcus searched the men's faces and stopped at his boss. "Frankie, you gotta listen to me."

"Shut up, Marcus," Frankie said and kicked him in the side, too.

He coughed and curled into a ball to protect himself, but they were done kicking him. This was too public, too exposed.

They lifted him up and carried him to the back door by the garage. Their strength impressed him. He weighed a hundred and seventy-plus pounds, and the two bikers who moved him into the house treated him like he weighed nothing more than a heavy sack of potatoes.

In the kitchen, they dropped him on the floor and stood guard, one man on either side. He looked up at them and rolled, trying to see Frankie, but couldn't.

"Make sure he doesn't leave your sight," the leader said from another room.

Marcus leaned up and rested his back against the cupboard under the sink. Neither biker stopped him.

What would Frankie have under the sink to use as a weapon? Was there something in there he could spray in their faces? Where were the knives Frankie cooked with? What part of the counter?

After a minute, the head biker entered the kitchen with Frankie in tow. Frankie went for his cigarette, but it had gone out.

"Hey, Frankie, that back door locked?"

Frankie looked at the head biker. "Yeah, why?"

"I don't want this asshole," he gestured at Marcus, "getting away again. He's a slippery fuck."

Frankie turned to Marcus, a new cigarette in his fingers, the matches ready to light. "Why'd you do it?"

"Do what?" Marcus asked. "I didn't do anything. These leather-bound posers stole from you. I was just working late that night." A moment of clarity struck him. For the first time since it all began, he actually felt something was right with what he had just said. "I was just working. They came in and killed Katy." Marcus shook his head at the futility of it all. "She was just there to pick me up, and now she's dead." He locked eyes with Frankie. "You should've listened to me a minute ago."

"Why?" Frankie asked. "What do you have to say?"

"They're going to kill you, too."

"Yeah, right." Frankie struck the match and brought the flame to his cigarette. After he puffed twice, he blew the smoke skyward and tossed the match into an ashtray. "I made a deal a long time ago."

"I know all about it," Marcus said. "To fix things, to make things right, you manage the store for the consortium. That's it. Your weekend jail visits are over, and now you're on your last payments, and it's all over. Someone else will come in to run the store. I know how it all works, but you're wrong, Frankie. It is over, but not in the way you think. He's," Marcus pointed at the head biker, "here to kill you in your own kitchen. Bullet to the forehead. I came back to warn you."

The two thugs standing over him guffawed as if he was making stupid jokes over a couple of beers.

Frankie pulled on his smoke again, the expression on his face lacking certainty. "Came back from where? Tell me, Marcus, where did you come back from?"

"The future. I saw him kill you. In this kitchen."

They all laughed. The head biker was doing something behind Frankie, but Marcus couldn't see what it was.

"Frankie," he shouted.

"That's rich, Marcus," Frankie said. "You almost had me there. How could you rob my store, kill your own woman, and then come here for more?" He stopped. The men quieted down. "Hey, that sorta rhymed," he added and spun around. The head biker had a black gun aimed at Frankie's forehead.

The two men watching him had diverted their attention to their boss.

Marcus leaned forward, got on his knees before anyone noticed, and launched off the floor.

But he was too late.

Frankie's head jerked back at the loud report of the weapon.

Marcus screamed as he hit the head biker in the midsection. The gun flew from his hand as they landed on the end of the solid oak table. The tough biker didn't grunt or moan. All he did was play limp for a moment, waiting for his men to step in and do their magic.

By the time Marcus righted himself and lifted a fist to do any damage, the two men yanked him off their boss and threw him against the wall beside the table.

He fell and slumped beside Frankie's twitching body.

The gun!

"You okay, Henry?" one of the bikers asked their leader.

Henry? That's a biker's name? Seriously?

The gun was two feet away. Marcus had never fired a weapon before, but he figured he could learn quickly.

He pushed off the wall with his feet and lunged for the gun, keeping his body under the kitchen table for protection. The gun's handle was warm in his grasp. He spun it around, brought the barrel up, and aimed it at the face of the man who had been the unfortunate one to bend down to look at what Marcus was doing.

The recoil jammed his hand back, straining his wrist, as the bullet spit out the end. The man's face opened up just above his eyes, a gaping hole between the eyebrows. He moaned something unintelligible and fell sideways.

Marcus had no idea how many bullets were in the gun. What he did know was that the power had shifted into his hands. These men had killed Katy and killed Frankie. These men had robbed his store and hurt him. Without the ability to travel through time, Katy and everything he had lost would be true because these men cared nothing for human life.

So at that moment, Marcus cared nothing for their life. He fired at the legs of the two remaining men in the kitchen from one foot away. After two bullets were pumped into one man and two into the other, he crawled out from under the table amid the shouting and wailing of the two men left alive.

The biker who had guarded him on the kitchen floor just a few minutes ago had a gun in his hand and fumbled with something on it as he leaned against the countertop for support.

Marcus fired from four feet away. Half of the man's neck opened in a spray of arterial blood. His body went limp and slid off the side of the countertop.

The leader begged. "Okay, okay, you win. We can talk about this —"

Marcus fired the weapon at the man's mouth to shut him up. The bullet stopped his pleading and tore a large hole through his cheek. He moaned and rolled away. Marcus put the gun to the back of the biker's skull and fired again.

The gun clicked empty.

He dropped fast, grabbed the other biker's weapon, and without thinking, pulled its trigger, but nothing happened.

He frantically looked for safety as the man groaned and tried to crawl away but couldn't figure out how to make the gun work. Frustrated, Marcus tossed the gun aside, knowing none of this would matter after returning to Friday and quitting his job. Katy would be alive, and he wouldn't have killed anyone.

But when he looked at the man crawling away, all he saw and felt was a wild rage for the man who had placed him in a barred stall with the body of his beloved. Knowing no one would ever see this, and he would never have to pay for his crimes, Marcus walked over to the counter, selected the largest knife out of Frankie's knife block, and followed the blood trail out of the kitchen and down the hall.

The head biker was tougher than he thought. Two bullets in his leg and a large chunk of his face missing, yet he could still get out of the kitchen, down the hall, and make it as far as five feet away from the front door.

"Wow, I'm impressed," Marcus said. "You're a tough one."

He pushed the man down with his foot. Then he swung the knife and brought it down across the right hamstring of the biker. It sliced through his clothes easily, through his leg, and nicked into the wood of the floor.

"Oops, sorry, Frankie. But don't worry. I'll get that damaged floor cleaned up as soon as I return to Friday."

He slashed with the knife again and again without realizing how many times.

After five minutes, completely spent and covered in blood, he dropped to the floor and slipped into the wet crimson mess that seemed to be everywhere.

He leaned against the side of Frankie's hallway armchair and panted, surveying his handiwork.

The biker wasn't recognizable anymore. A slab of ripped and torn clothing was mixed with white bone and red goop all over the corridor. The only real piece recognizable was his head, which had rolled a few feet away from his disarranged body.

When he was back in the barn, the smell of his loving, caring, decaying Katy caused something inside to snap and stay broken. The pain was too much to handle, and from that moment forward, nothing, not even time travel, could undo any of it.

Plunging the knife into the man who had caused this hell was a pleasure he had never thought possible. It was so euphoric he wanted to do it again and again.

But now it was time to leave. Probably the most pleasurable part of this massacre was that he knew it would be erased as soon as he went back further in time. Everything will be fixed on Friday. All would be forgiven because it hadn't even happened.

And maybe he could give Frankie a parting gift when he quit on Friday. He could leave him a note detailing the consortium's plans for his departure.

Maybe. Maybe not.

He got off the floor, dropped the knife in the chunks of warm meat, and walked to the guest bathroom he had used at another time, on work events and barbecues.

After cleaning himself up, he was pleased to see that he wasn't bleeding anywhere.

Perfect.

Time to travel.

In the living room, he sat on the couch and closed his eyes.

Someone knocked on the front door.

His earlier self was here. He briefly wondered what would happen now. His earlier self wouldn't be taken to the barn in Orangeville because the bikers were dead. His earlier self wouldn't even get inside the house.

A police siren wailed in the distance.

A neighbor must have heard the gunfire and called 911.

His earlier self knocked again.

A buzzer wailed somewhere.

Commotion reigned, and the Marcus on the couch disappeared.

Chapter 20

SUDDENLY, AS IF HE'D traveled too many times, it all came rushing back, racing by his consciousness. The illuminated and overlapping realities slammed him back into the couch. Then he was on a chair, in a bush, out of a bush, on the barn floor, and at the back of his father's yard.

As his soul ripped through the last twelve hours of traveling, he was conscious of each whoosh of air, each intake of the people he passed, and felt every bang and bump.

His panic grew as he was dragged back through time, knowing the first place he had traveled from was the interrogation room. At any moment, he was about to drop into the locked room, his wrists bound to the table. If that happened, he would have to travel again. It was nothing to be concerned about. But with each pull, his fear intensified.

The whooshing got louder, the speed faster.

Then, for whatever reason, he was slammed back into the chair in the interrogation room, cuffed and alone at the table as if he had never left.

***

Detective Green's cell phone rang.

"Green."

"Um, Detective, you're not going to believe this."

"Who is this?"

"Detective Wisson. You know, three cubicles from you on the second floor."

"Right, I know you. What won't I believe?"

They had left Spinoza on the lawn of Frankie's house, the massacre brutal. From the clothing alone, Spinoza had determined that three members of the Spawns biker gang were slaughtered along with Frankie, Marcus's boss. The guy dusting the gun for prints found one set. They would have more on the print within the hour.

"Well?" he asked. "You called me, Wisson. What is it?"

"You're looking for that guy that walked out of the interrogation room on you, right? Marcus, something?"

"Yeah." He snuck a look at Smith. "Marcus Johnson."

"Well, guess what?"

"What?" Green was tired of the games. "Spit it out."

He flicked his blinker and merged onto the highway, dropped the accelerator, and pressed the phone into his ear.

"You know that interrogation room with the defective door?"

"Of course I do. Intimately."

"Inside that room is Marcus Johnson, sitting in the chair, cuffed to the table."

Green looked at Smith, eyes wide. Smith watched him, gesturing with his hands to know what was happening.

"You're fucking with me. Impossible."

"No. I'm not. I'm looking at him through the two-way glass right now. No joke. He's sitting there as clear as day."

"What, he just decided to play nicey nice and walk back in

undetected, sit down and cuff himself to the table?"

"Unbelievable, I know. But I'm looking right at him."

"I'm on my way, but if you're fucking with—"

"Don't believe me then."

"Make sure he doesn't walk away again."

The phone clicked off.

"You're not going to believe this," Green said as he slammed the accelerator all the way to the floor and flipped the lights and siren on.

***

He sweated, he cried, and he prayed. Nothing worked. He couldn't move. He had no idea why, but his traveling days appeared to be over.

Maybe it was for the better. If the cops were in a good mood, they would listen. He could concoct a story. One that would be believable. One that would work.

He waited for someone to enter the room. He needed to use the bathroom to clean up. Some of the biker's blood was still covering his arms.

It felt like an hour had passed before the door burst open.

The two detectives from the hospital were back. The look in their eyes was surprise, shock.

"Hey guys," Marcus said. "Think I could get a bathroom break here. You've had me in here all day. Where did you guys go all this time? Hungry, too. You guys got any food?"

They looked at each other, then back at him.

A third officer stepped into the room.

"Who's this?" Marcus asked.

"I'm Detective Wisson. I'm here to verify to these two men that they're not just seeing things. State your name and date of birth, please."

"Marcus Johnson, date of birth is the month of your ass and the date of fuck you. The year is bestiality. Now, bathroom break or not?"

All three detectives exchanged looks.

Green pointed at the glass. "Wisson, make sure that thing is rolling. We got it from here."

Wisson backed out of the room, and the door clicked shut.

"Marcus, do you want to tell us where you've been?" Detective Green asked. He pulled out a chair on the opposite side of the metal table and sat down. Smith walked to the corner, crossed his arms, and leaned against the wall.

Green tapped the table as if he was nervous.

"Oh man, if you only knew," Marcus said.

"Tell us. We want to help."

"I'm a time traveler."

The lines on Green's forehead intensified when he raised his eyebrows. He looked at Smith and then at his fingers as if formulating his next question.

"Start at the beginning," Green said.

"Bathroom first. That's where we start. That's the beginning. Otherwise, suck me."

"This choice of language. Where does one pick that up? The store you worked?"

"The John, the toilet, washroom, bathroom, restroom, the loo, el banjo, la toilette, water closet. Which language would you understand because English doesn't seem to be taking?"

"You can use the toilet in good time. Right now, you're not leaving my sight." He stopped tapping and took his hand off the table. "Now, tell us, what have you been up to?"

Marcus released his bladder. It didn't matter anymore. If he couldn't go back to Friday, Katy was dead for real, and he would rot in prison for the murder of those three bikers and his boss. He killed them in self-defense, but he also knew he could go back to Friday. He did it for Katy. But what scared him the most was he had enjoyed it.

He had killed those men with pleasure.

Urine slipped down his leg and pooled under his chair. It took a moment for the two detectives to catch on. Green sniffed the air. His nose twisted, and he moaned.

"You asshole," Green said. "What did you do?"

"I warned you. Now you can sit in the piss of your discontent."

"Wrong. You can sit in your own piss." He got up from his chair and opened the door. "Smith, let's go."

They stepped into the hallway and slammed the door, leaving Marcus alone to focus.

All he had to do was meditate hard enough, and he would be gone.

He closed his eyes and thought about Friday.

***

"I'll watch the door, so he doesn't leave. Run up to our desks and grab a bottle of Vick's Vapor Rub."

"Are you kidding?"

"I'm not letting him out of our sight. They can clean him up when we're done, and we'll stick him behind bars. But for now, he isn't going anywhere until his arraignment in the morning, and even then, no judge in his right mind will let this one walk."

Smith ran off upstairs and returned in under five minutes.

They applied the Vicks directly under their noses and opened the door to the interrogation room.

Marcus Johnson was gone.

For a brief second, Green didn't breathe.

Then Marcus lifted his head up from under the table. He had bent over far enough to be unseen from the door.

"Boo," he yelled.

Involuntarily, Green jumped an inch at the volume Marcus used.

"Gotcha." He smiled.

They entered the room. Neither detective took a seat.

"You want to start by telling us whose blood is on your arms?"

"Filthy bikers."

Green couldn't believe how easy this was. A virtual confession and he hadn't been officially charged with anything, so he had no Miranda rights and no lawyer. This was going to be an open-and-shut case.

"What bikers?" he asked.

"The Spawns of Hell club."

"Are you referring to the Spawns Motorcycle Club?"

Marcus nodded. "They robbed my store Sunday night. Katy came to take me out after work." He looked up at Green, his eyes pleading. "They killed her and stashed her body at their clubhouse off Highway 9, near Orangeville. An old barn." He broke down, shoulders heaving. "She's rotting in their barn, and there's nothing I can do about it."

Green had to take a moment to comprehend what he was hearing. He looked at Smith, and the expression on his face was mystified, blown away.

He waited for Marcus to collect himself enough to talk again. After a minute, he did.

"I visited my dad to ask his advice, and he told me to talk to Frankie because he would want to hear the truth about what had happened at the store. After what you guys said when we were here earlier today and at my house, I didn't think Frankie would listen to me unless I got to him first. Frankie explained to me that a consortium owns his store and that this company rules everything. They had the bikers burn him for the cash. Then they showed up at Frankie's and shot him. I jumped the head biker to escape, knocking the gun from him. To save my life, I shot them and had to use the knife on the one crawling away. I killed them, sure," Marcus said, spittle falling from his lips, his eyes bloodshot, "but in self-defense. Then I came in here and sat down so you could hear everything from me. I've done nothing wrong. I'm innocent, and the bad people are dead."

He broke down, his forehead resting on the table.

Green and Smith waited.

Marcus whispered something.

"What was that?" Green asked in a soft voice.

"I said—" Marcus coughed and cleared his throat. "But Katy's still dead. And for some reason, I can't go back in time to fix that."

Green moved toward the door and nodded for Smith to join him. They exited quietly and shut the door as Marcus's sobs increased.

They walked next door and entered the camera room, where Wisson sat in the corner watching the interrogation room.

"If what he's saying is true, there's no case against him here," Green said. "He might walk after all this."

Wisson nodded. "Holy shit, man."

"Exactly."

"But," Smith said, "who would believe him? He evades custody all day, runs from the police, and kills four men. We have Katy's blood all over his house and his prints on the knife."

Green's phone rang. He held up a finger. "It's Spinoza."

He punched a button. "Yeah?"

"The prints came back on the gun," Spinoza said.

"And?"

"They're Marcus's. Have you found him yet?"

"Got him right here," Green said.

"Where's here?"

"The interrogation room he walked out of earlier."

"You're kidding?"

"No. I'm not."

"I'm on my way."

"No need. He just confessed to murdering all those men. Except for Frankie. He says the bikers offed Frankie."

"Whatever. Be there soon."

Green shut his phone.

"Prints?" Smith asked.

Green nodded. "Marcus's."

"There's the case."

Green shrugged. "Looks like it. Hey, anyone get a hold of his support group?"

"Yeah, the head of the group, Samuel Levy, is on his way down to talk to Marcus. Actually," he looked at his watch. "He's probably here already. I'll get him down here. After all that Marcus has been through and what he's about to have to deal with, maybe having Samuel here will help him."

"Deal. Go get the friend. That's better than a lawyer any day of the week."

They laughed and patted each other on the shoulder. This case wrapped up faster and easier than either of them had expected. No one would have to go before any disciplinary hearings.

"Wrap it up," Green said and left the room.

Chapter 21

THEY HAD LEFT HIM in the interrogation room long enough. He'd stayed, given them a chance to hear his story, and now they were sweating him.

But for what?

He could simply focus and then be gone at any time. Sure, he had trouble getting back to Friday, but maybe if he really tried, he could get back to Sunday afternoon before closing the store.

Maybe if he tried hard enough, he could do anything.

Marcus closed his eyes and focused on Friday. After a couple of minutes with no success, he shook his head, cleared those thoughts, and focused on Sunday afternoon. That shouldn't be too hard. Sunday was only yesterday. Before the blood. Before the robbery.

Just as he was about to leave the interrogation room, he thought he heard Samuel's voice outside the door.

He pulled back and listened.

That was Samuel Levy, for sure.

What's he doing here?

He wondered if Samuel still had his Paris picture. If he did, maybe that would be one more piece of the story that the police would believe. The picture would surely help him at this time.

Or at least he could tell the police that Marcus had disappeared right in front of him when he traveled to Frankie's street the first time. With Samuel's testimony, they had to believe him.

So it was okay to leave now. With him gone, the police would understand as Samuel recounted what he knew to be true.

Samuel had come to help him. To save him.

Marcus smiled. He knew he could count on Samuel.

He went back to the task of meditating to travel home on Sunday afternoon.

A moment later, he disappeared.

Chapter 22

Marcus materialized in his bed; the covers ruffled from a good night's sleep.

He smiled, sighed, and stared up at the ceiling. The scent of bacon and eggs drifted in the air.

The nightmare was over. This had to be Sunday. Or Friday. Whichever, it didn't matter to him. Either day worked.

He had done it. Erased everything. He wrapped his arms up over his head and wept. Katy was downstairs and not rotting in a barn near Orangeville. Everything was right with the world again.

He rolled onto his side and let the tears flow. Loving another human being this much hurts. Katy had come into his life, heard his story, and loved him anyway. She had cared so much about him that she studied Alzheimer's disease and how to deal with it once it was diagnosed. It was her idea to attend the support group years before any symptoms were evident. That way, his mind would be exercised, his awareness heightened, and his sense of caring and community would forever be with him. Even as he lost his ability to remember things or cope with everyday life, the support group would still be there.

All that because she loved him. Her mandate had always been to support him, and his was Katy.

He loved her beyond anything he could ever describe. If the sun disappeared, he would light her way. If a madman stood in the room with one bullet in his gun, he would take that bullet for her. It would be an honor. There was nothing that could quell his love and devotion for Katy, and she knew it. But that was the kind of woman Katy was. She reveled in that knowledge. To be wanted, to be cherished. She had always dreamed of that, and he made her dreams come true.

He rolled over and sat up on the edge of the bed. The morning sunshine cast its glow across the bedroom floor.

There was no blood anywhere in the room.

Carefully, he raised a hand to his cheek to feel for the gash on his face from the night of the robbery. His cheek was clean, his skin undamaged.

Soft tissue from an old scar was in the same area, but that didn't matter as long as there was no bandage or blood.

He wondered what had happened to Detective Green and Smith. Since Marcus traveled back in time to before the robbery, they wouldn't even know his name.

That meant the bikers were still alive.

And Frankie.

He would deal with Frankie at a later date. Right now, he wanted to go downstairs, have breakfast, hold his woman for as long as he could, and leave time travel well enough alone.

It had benefited him thus far, but he was done with it. Only in extreme cases would he travel again. And only if he needed to.

He traveled with his clothes each and every time, but when he looked down, he was dressed in white pants and a white shirt. The look made him laugh. It was as if he had been in a hospital or something.

At least he didn't have the piss all over him from the interrogation room.

In the corner of the room sat a new red chair.

When did Katy get that?

He hadn't seen it the other night. Maybe he'd been too tired to notice. He did get in late Monday morning after they had stitched him up.

He headed for the door. Something else caught his eye. At the door, he stopped and turned around. The bedroom itself was different. Everything was different. The headboard had changed, and the covers on the bed. Even the giant stuffed giraffe in the corner was new.

Could he have gone back a month, six months? Did he go back and change the future, and now he needed to get used to it?

The white bed sheets had a small red mark where he had sat on them. He looked down at his white pants and found a bloody mark on the backside.

That's strange. Why is my ass bleeding?

He touched himself and then withdrew his hand. Nothing seemed to be bleeding now. Maybe a little blood came through with him when he traveled somehow. It didn't matter, though. He was back, and so was Katy.

He entered the bathroom to wash his hands for breakfast. Today was going to be an amazing day. After breakfast, they would go to the park for a walk. Then an afternoon nap with her special request, kisses on the neck and back, a massage, and finally, mind-blowing sex. Yeah, today, he would make love to the woman of his dreams and make sure she understood the definition of the word goddess. After all he had gone through, his newfound appreciation for Katy was abundant.

The bathroom was subtly different, too. The toothbrushes were in a cup. They never did that. The toilet had a tiny carpet in front of it and a plush blue cover on the lid. Since when did Katy decorate like that?

But none of that mattered. Actually, it made sense. It worked with how different the bedroom was. Whatever he had done with time travel or however far back he had gone, it would all work out.

Because Katy was alive, and nothing else mattered.

He turned to read the plaque on the wall as he dried his hands, the one dedicated to their relationship, but it wasn't there. A picture with toilet humor graced the wall where their love statement once sat.

What the fuck is that?

No way would Katy take that plaque down. Not in a million years. She loved that plaque. It meant everything to them as a couple.

Unless she moved it to the bedroom or kitchen. He nodded to the face in the mirror. It had to be in the kitchen.

Eggs and bacon, then locate the plaque. Life in order. That's what he needed. Life in order.

A woman started singing in the kitchen, her voice angelic. He had never heard Katy sing like that before.

It made him smile as he skipped from the bathroom and headed down the stairs. At the bottom, near the front foyer, he stopped. The living room was also different. Not just the furniture but the arrangement as well.

What's going on?

For a moment, his stomach protested. This was too much. If Katy had redecorated the house, wouldn't he have been a part of the decision process? If so, wouldn't his current self be aware of what he was looking at? Unless the Early Onset Alzheimer's had set in. But he hadn't been diagnosed. Nothing had changed. Days ago, he was working at The Act of Love. The robbery, the police, and everything that went with it happened, and he got away, thanks to his mother's gift from before he was born.

Therefore, everything had a logical explanation.

He walked the length of the hallway toward the kitchen with the understanding that the table and chairs would probably be all new as well.

At the kitchen door, he put a hand on the doorframe and waited, bracing himself for the sight of Katy alive after holding her dead hand on the barn floor. He needed a deep breath to steady himself. The last thing he wanted was to barge into the kitchen, see her, and fall to his knees.

The angelic singing had stopped.

It was time. He took a deep breath, stepped into the kitchen, and fainted.

***

When he woke, several men stood over him. One of the men held a needle in his hand.

No, not the needle. Samuel Levy always brought the needle. Never the needle again.

He spun sideways and tried to scramble away. Hands grabbed at him, but in his panic, he proved stronger.

When he had entered the kitchen, a man had Katy over the counter and was doing things to her. He fainted like a baby instead of attacking the man and saving his Katy. How could he ever be considered her hero if he didn't save her?

The hands grabbing at him found purchase, yanking him back to the center of the kitchen floor.

The needle plunged into his thigh. Almost instantly, a lightness of being coursed through him, and a calm, peaceful, easy feeling caused him to cease his struggle.

People talked around him. About him.

"I don't know," a woman's voice said. "I was cooking breakfast. My husband was in the kitchen with me. The next thing I know,

Marcus walked in and fainted on the floor. This has to stop. We can't keep living like this—"

"She's right," a man's voice. "This is our house now. We bought it a year ago. Haven't you got any security measures at your hospital? Can't you keep this one locked up?"

"Yes," someone else said.

Then another man said, "We're so sorry this happened. We'll take measures so that it never happens again. Believe me."

"That's what the one before you said."

"I'm so sorry. We'll leave now and do everything we can to stop this."

"I'm warning you. If he so much as comes onto my property again, I may have to take security measures into my own hands."

"Which is your right. You have to protect your home and your family. But I assure you, this one won't see the light of day for a while."

"And why is he bleeding back there?"

"We're not sure. Maybe it has to do with his condition."

"Please, just leave. Take Marcus with you and leave us alone."

"Consider us gone."

The hands were on him again. He tried to travel, but nothing worked because of whatever was in that needle. He couldn't concentrate or focus.

That horrible needle.

Gets me every time.

Then he went under.

Chapter 23

JERALD JOHNSON SAT IN the waiting lounge at the hospital. He struggled to contain his anger, his pain. The inability to protect his child from being the father he always wanted to be. The rage became a vessel of poison, eating at him.

That was how he justified murder.

The man responsible for hurting Marcus and causing everything to go wrong in his life was dead.

His son had taught him that murder cleansed the soul. Right a wrong, clean the slate, put the mantlepiece back on the hearth where it belonged. You don't reward the rapist and hurt the raped. It had to be the other way around. No one understood that basic human need to filter the toxic people from their life.

Jerald did. And he had no problem being the filter, even if that meant filtering toxicity for his son, as he couldn't do it on his own anymore.

That brought life full circle. Now, as his son lived with the debilitating disease of Alzheimer's, his father could protect him.

"Mr. Johnson." Doctor Simmons stepped in front of Jerald. "So glad you could make it."

"I wouldn't miss it for the world."

Jerald wiped at the tears that fell from his cheeks.

"I'm sorry," the doctor said. "This must be hard for you, considering everything that's happened."

He allowed the doctor to think his tears were ones of sorrow.

Fuck him and all doctors for what they let happen to Marcus. No one hurts my boy with impunity.

"Follow me to my office. We'll talk first. Then we'll go see Marcus."

The doctor led the way, meandering through the labyrinthine halls of the care clinic where Marcus had been placed after the lengthy murder trial two years ago.

After being charged with multiple murders, a year in court, and psychological assessments, Marcus Johnson was sentenced to this psychiatric hospital for the rest of his days and diagnosed as paranoid schizophrenic. That, plus the Early Onset Alzheimer's Disease showed signs of setting in, Marcus couldn't recall many details of his whereabouts during those horrific hours when Katy was murdered.

The system failed him. The jury failed him. Everyone failed him.

But his father wouldn't. Never again.

They entered Simmons's office, where he gestured for Jerald to take a seat.

"As you're aware, I called you here today because your son asked to see you."

This time a tear of sorrow fell. One of pain and loss.

"He has these rare moments of absolute lucidity where he talks with an uncharacteristic clarity."

"What has he been saying?"

The doctor shrugged. "Some of the usual stuff about the trial, the bikers, and his old boss, Frankie. He talks about Katy a lot."

"Is that why he broke out two weeks ago? You know, when he was caught in the kitchen of the house he used to share with Katy? Was he talking about her then?"

The doctor nodded. "As you know, Alzheimer's causes difficulty in remembering recent events. Symptoms include confusion," the doctor pulled one finger down after another as he recited the list, "irritability, aggression, mood swings, and eventually long-term memory loss." The doctor lowered his hands.

Jerald didn't move. He didn't blink.

"Life expectancy after the Alzheimer's diagnosis is typically seven years, but we assume that Marcus was already two or more years in when he was diagnosed."

"What are you saying?"

"This is only speculation, but I think Katy saw the signs all those years ago and got him involved in that support group offered at the hospital." The doctor pushed his chair back and stood up. He walked to the window and gazed out at the city of Toronto. "Pity what happened to Samuel Levy, dying the way he did. Brutal murder." He stopped, waited for a heartbeat, then added, "I'm sorry to hear you were brought in for questioning on that."

"They have to cover all the bases. Since my son was one of his victims, and Samuel was charged after Marcus escaped him weeks ago, they had to talk to me. I was hosting a fundraiser for Alzheimer's disease sixty miles from the site of the murder in downtown Toronto. Seven hundred people saw me on stage as Samuel was killed at that event. It was impossible for me to have been anywhere near him. So, now the police have their work cut out for them, so to speak."

The doctor turned around. "You sound upset, bitter."

"Wouldn't you be? You find out your son has been violated for three years, and to escape it, his mind went places unheard of, as anyone's would. The difference for Marcus is he's the ultimate victim because of his condition. I understand that's why Samuel founded the support group. So he could prey on people whose memories couldn't be trusted in a court of law."

The doctor sighed. "That's what they were saying, but none of that really matters now."

Dr. Simmons picked up a file from the corner of his desk and flipped it open.

"What's that?" Jerald asked.

"The psychological assessments of your son." The doctor looked up. "Are you aware of what paranoid schizophrenic actually means?"

"No, but I'm sure you'll tell me."

If the doctor noticed the sarcasm, he didn't let on.

"It just means a breakdown of thought that includes delusions and disorganized thinking, which include auditory hallucinations. He becomes paranoid from bizarre delusions and disorganized speech. We call that a 'word salad' in severe cases."

"That's not Marcus."

"In your opinion. Professionals have assessed him. That's why he's in our care and not in prison serving a life sentence."

It was clear to Jerald that Dr. Simmons preferred to rely on his colleagues' work rather than the father's opinion, who knew Marcus to be of sound mind, minus what Alzheimer's was doing to him.

"A paranoid schizophrenic also maintains sloppy dress, which means they can be found going barefoot everywhere. At the beginning of Marcus's trial, he was discovered barefoot several times."

Jerald waited for the point as he was sure the doctor was leading him somewhere.

Dr. Simmons closed the file and set it back on the desk. "What I'm trying to illustrate is that your son has shown remarkable progress in recent days. Actually, it's been ever since he heard of Samuel's death."

"That has to tell you something."

"But this talk of time travel hasn't stopped."

"When I see him, I'll discuss it with him."

The doctor looked concerned. "Would you? He's scaring the others. They've seen him in their rooms after they've gone to bed. Their doors were locked. We've searched Marcus's room and cannot locate any master keys. I don't know how he keeps escaping, either. I can't for the life of me understand how he does it unless someone is helping him."

"You mean someone who works here?"

"That's my thought."

"Mine too."

"As an aside, please understand that Marcus has been through something extremely traumatic. In order to cope with what was happening to him, he escaped mentally. He said he traveled through time, going to many places. The weekend when Katy and the bikers were killed, was the same weekend he had a support group meeting. It makes sense to us that that was how he coped. But now that it's over, it would be best for everyone here if he calmed some of his rhetoric down." They sat in silence for a moment. The doctor raised a finger and added, "Let's go see him. I'm sure he's ready for you now."

Jerald followed Dr. Simmons back through the long, winding corridors until they came to Marcus's door.

"I'll bring you in and introduce you unless he remembers you. After you're settled, I'll leave you two alone to chat."

Simmons knocked, then unlocked the door. He opened it slowly and stepped in. Jerald followed.

Marcus sat in a wooden chair by the window. His room was on the second floor, offering a view of the orange leaves on the autumn trees. He didn't move or acknowledge the door opening.

"Marcus?" the doctor said in a soft voice. "I've brought someone here to see you. Are you up to having a visitor?"

Marcus whispered something.

"What was that, Marcus? I couldn't hear you."

Marcus turned to them. When he did, Jerald saw recognition in his son's eyes. "I asked if you brought Katy with you."

"No, unfortunately, Katy isn't here today. But your father is."

Marcus swiveled back to the window.

The doctor shrugged as if to apologize. "He was better earlier when I called you."

"I can hear you," Marcus said. "I'm fine. Please leave my father and me alone to talk."

The doctor backed out of the room and closed the door.

Marcus got up from his chair, turned to his father, and nearly fell back down. His face scrunched as his eyes filled with tears. He rushed across the floor, wrapped his arms around his father, and wept.

Jerald held him tight and wept along with him.

"I'm so sorry, son. I only wish I knew."

He waited for Marcus to get himself back under a semblance of control until they pulled away.

Marcus wiped at his face and grabbed a Kleenex to blow his nose.

They sat on the end of the bed together.

"No one ever believed me," Marcus said. "They all thought I killed Katy."

"I know, but I believe you."

"Those bikers robbed me that night. They hurt Katy and left the store. Sure I took her home. It's where she ought to be. But they came that morning and stole her body to remove any evidence of their involvement."

"It was a crazy time for everyone. Even me."

"After it was all said and done, those three bikers deserved what they got. It was self-defense, but they deserved it."

"I agree, as did Samuel. If anyone deserved it more, it was him."

"I know. Whoever did that to Samuel is an angel."

Jerald stared at him hard and winked.

"You?" Marcus asked. "But how? You were at the fundraiser. At least that's what they told me."

"I was at the fundraiser."

"Did you hire someone?" Marcus asked, his voice low like they were talking about a conspiracy.

Jerald reached into his pocket and pulled a photo out. "Remember this?"

Marcus took the photo and examined it. His bloodshot eyes watered again. "This was taken from me all those years ago by Samuel. You and Mom are at that café in Paris with Mom waving in the background." He looked up at his father. "How did you get this?"

"Who took the picture?" Jerald asked.

"I have no idea. The book Mom gave me didn't say anything about —" He stopped, looked at the photo, and then back at his father. "You?"

Jerald nodded. "Your mother didn't want to do any time traveling alone. She secretly brought me to the labs. We traveled back in time together. I'm the one who took that photo."

As Marcus's mind worked, Jerald saw it on his face. "And that's how you were at the fundraiser when Samuel was murdered. And the police say two men chased the murderer and cornered him, but he disappeared." Marcus met his cycs. "That was you?"

Jerald nodded. "I only wish I could've done it sooner. But we can't travel back more than a day or so. Otherwise, I would go all the way back to when you met this monster and destroy him then." Jerald wiped at a tear of his own. "I'm sorry I wasn't there for you, Marcus, but I am now."

Marcus got up, walked to the chair where he sat, and looked out the window again. "It's okay, Dad. You did what was needed. Now I can have peace."

"There's something else, isn't there?"

Marcus looked at him. "Yes."

"What is it? Can I do anything? I owe you for the lost years."

"There's nothing you can do for me."

"Try me."

"Katy."

"What about her?"

"She's all I want. She's all I ever wanted. And you know what's wonderful about losing your mind?"

"What?"

"Is that I can visit her whenever I want. She's always here with me."

That didn't sit right with Jerald. He didn't want to hear how his son was going crazy. Nothing of his son's condition was good. The man was only thirty-one years old. He was still at the beginning of his life, and yet they had him locked up in this place because he told the truth about his ability. They called it hallucinations, voices. The air whooshing when he returned to the current time really got to them. Whoosh was a national headline in major newspapers across the country after that. The 'whoosh trial' and 'whooshed right to jail.' They had been talking about his son, but that didn't stop the media from harassing him with questions about Marcus's upbringing and what caused a man to kill his own girlfriend and then kill bikers and try to frame them for everything.

Jerald hated those dark days and was quite happy it was all over.

But to hear his son acknowledge that his mind was slipping sounded like someone was coaching him, feeding him bullshit. Marcus had at least five more years left, two or three of them decent years.

"Dad, I need to be alone for a while."

"Okay, Marcus," Jerald said. He got up and walked to the door.

"Everything okay?"

"Sure. Katy's here. I'm happy again."

Jerald gripped the door handle until his knuckles whitened. "Okay, son, say hi to her for me."

"I will, Dad. Oh, and …" Marcus swiveled in his chair, the photo of the Paris café still in his grip. "Thanks for what you did for me. It was long overdue."

"No one will ever hurt you again, son. I'm here for you and will be here for the rest of it."

"I understand. And Dad?"

"Yeah?"

"I love you."

Jerald hadn't heard those words from his son in years. "I love you, too, Marcus."

A cloud moved in front of the sun outside, causing the room to darken. Marcus's face darkened with it.

"You did the right thing all those years ago, Marcus. I would've done the same. I'm so sorry that man hurt you."

"I'm sorry, too, Dad. I guess I learned how to deal with it. But Katy's here, and we need to talk. I want to show her the picture of you and Mom in Paris."

"I understand. Goodbye, son."

Marcus waved. Jerald waved.

Then he stepped out and closed the door.

He made it to his car before he broke down. Jerald drove out of the hospital's parking lot a half hour later when he felt it was safe to drive.

He looked up at Marcus's second-floor window on the way out of the lot and raised a hand to salute his son, a true warrior. His son, the man who fought for his woman. The man who killed those responsible. The man who taught his father the value of life.

And death.

Chapter 24

Marcus stared out the window of his room. He watched his father get to his car and continued watching until his father drove away.

When he was alone and the sky had clouded over, he looked at Katy lying in bed.

She opened her arms in invitation.

He smiled and walked to her.

"I love you, Katy."

"Get in the bed, silly, and hold me." Katy's smile warmed him. "I want to cuddle all afternoon."

Marcus pulled the covers back and got under them, snuggling up to Katy.

"My dad brought me a picture."

"I know. I saw it. Cool, eh, how they could do what you can do?" Katy snuggled closer. "That's why I love you so much, Marcus. Now, just hold me."

***

Dr. Simmons knocked on Marcus's door and used his key to open it. He stepped into the room and saw Marcus in bed.

"Your father left?"

Marcus didn't respond. He wrapped his arms around the pillow, holding it tight to his chest. It looked like he was upset about something.

"I'm sorry if I disturbed your nap," Simmons said. "It's just, I thought your father would come and see me before he left." Simmons shrugged. "Have a good nap, Marcus. I'll see you at dinner tonight in the cafeteria."

He backed out and closed the door.

***

Marcus held Katy tighter. It was rude of Dr. Simmons to just walk in. He was having private time with his woman. No one had the right to disturb that.

Maybe one day next week, he would have to teach Dr. Simmons a lesson about privacy. Maybe he would transport to his office naked and make him wonder how he did that.

In the meantime, he had Katy to cuddle. His beloved, his lifelong partner. His everything.

No one could take her away from him.

Katy was his, and he was Katy's.

Nothing else mattered when he was in Katy's arms.

Marcus turned the world off and held her for the rest of the day. He cried in her arms and was held by her, comforted.

In a single moment of understanding, he saw the pillow he held, rejected it, and prayed for God to take it away and give him his Katy or take his life and give him his Katy on the Other Side.

"Anything for Katy. My life for hers."

He held her harder.

"Anything for Katy."

Afterword

DEAR READER,

First dedication: my brother.

I will never forget the day we received the call that my brother, aged twenty, was missing. I was fourteen at the time, living in a suburb of Toronto, Ontario, and my brother was living in Calgary, Alberta.

It was 1984, late January, and my brother had taken a bus to Sunshine Village Ski Resort near Banff, Alberta. After that fateful day, he didn't show up for work, and a couple of days later, we received the call that he was missing.

Fifteen days later, in early February, my brother's body was found by a cadaver dog behind Sunshine Mountain, covered in snow, frozen solid. The dog found his skis first. Then at three in the afternoon on a Monday, the dog located my brother.

Some say that dying of hypothermia isn't such a bad way to go. The cold numbs your extremities first, then works its way deeper. You get so numb that you don't feel the pain anymore. You become delusional, can't walk well, and may even begin burrowing. Twenty to fifty percent of all victims who succumb to hypothermia often disrobe as the body tries one last time to heat itself. This is called paradoxical undressing. The victim is tricked into feeling not only warm but that they're boiling hot on the inside as muscles contract in a last attempt at maintaining life.

The pain of having a sibling missing for two weeks was almost unbearable. We all had theories. Ones that involved him being alive, even though the police informed us of the statistics, telling us we needed to prepare for the worst as each day he was missing dragged on.

The loss and anguish I felt when his body was discovered will haunt me forever. I still remember the phone ringing. I will always remember the phone ringing. I heard my mother's wail when she was told the news. To this day, I do not know how a parent can manage after having lost one of their babies, but my mother's a trooper. It took years, but somehow she managed.

I still weep for my brother at times. When I hear his favorite song, or wake from an intense dream where he's visited me in my home, had dinner with me.

Twenty years after his death on Sunshine Mountain, in March 2004, I flew to Calgary, rented a Cadillac, and drove out to Sunshine Village Ski Resort. I stayed three days at the Banff Springs Hotel and skied Sunshine. In honor of the brother, the son, the friend that Sunshine Mountain took from my family at such an early age, I went there and conquered the damn thing. I skied hard, whispered a silent tribute, and owned it for my brother. The mountain couldn't have the last word. Someone in my family had to replicate what my brother did and walk away. I did that, and Sunshine Mountain will never be the same. At least not for me.

The theory of time travel has always fascinated me. I love movies and books about it and have always wanted to write a novel on the subject.

So, I wrote this one because I wanted to be Marcus. I wanted to go back and talk my brother out of getting on that bus. I wanted to tell him to not go skiing that day because there would be too much snow coming down, that he won't be able to see where he was going, and that he would get lost. In minus temperatures, getting lost on the back of a mountain in Alberta is almost certain death.

I wanted to make things right.

But I couldn't.

And neither could Marcus.

The last time I saw my brother alive was August 1983. We talked briefly on the phone during Christmas later that year, then he got on a bus in late January and never came home.

We fought as youngsters.

It took years for me to recover from that. He was a good man. I have wonderful memories of him. I just wished I could've gone back and fixed things.

Now I live with no regrets. I learned a hard lesson. Treat people in a manner that you can walk away from. If they deserve your love, give it to them. If they deserve your anger, give it to them.

I miss you and always will.

Until I see you on the other side …

My second dedication: my parents.

The second part of this afterward is mostly for my dad. After my brother died and the funeral was over, days later, my dad got up and went back to work. I don't know how he did it, but he did.

Then he escaped with me over the years in movies. We watched *Death Wish* with Charles Bronson together. We watched *Omega Man*, *Salem's Lot*, and many more. Horrors, thrillers, and movies about time travel.

In a way, those early experiences and the novels I read (Stephen King et al., from grade six and on) made me who I am today.

Because of my father, to some degree, I am a writer.

To honor him, this book's release date was January 23rd, his birthday.

Also, during the investigation of my missing brother, one of the RCMP officers was named Detective Green. That's also my dad's name (he's a stepdad. There's a long story there). My father was a cop with the Toronto Police Department before I was born. He rode a Harley on the highways around Toronto. My father's last name is Green. I kept my last name from my mother's first marriage.

That's why there's Detective Green in this book.

Marcus's parents' favorite song was "Long Cool Woman in a Black Dress" by the Hollies. I used that song because it was the first song my parents danced to all those years ago when they met on that fateful night that would forever be the first day they set eyes on each other.

Both my parents are alive and well today (read the addendum below). They're survivors, having both come through cancer.

My dad has a room in his house called the Zombie Emporium where he watches horror movies (with me) and plays video games where he hunts zombies.

Finally, this novel came to be because of my desire to do something for my lost brother. But it also came together because of my parents.

To them, I say thank you.

To my brother, I say … see you one day, and when we do get together, we will have a lot of catching up to do.

"Life goes on," as he always said. It's written on his headstone at the cemetery where he is buried.

Rock on.

Jonas Saul

(Addendum: my mother passed away on August 22, 2017, after a massive stroke the day before. May she Rest in Peace)

About Jonas Saul

Jonas Saul is the bestselling author of the Sarah Roberts Series—more than two million sold!—and has written and published over sixty thrillers. After acquiring an agent, he signed several deals in Los Angeles, with MadRiver Pictures optioning his Sarah Roberts Series —over forty books!—(currently in development).

Jonas has often outranked Stephen King and Dean Koontz on Amazon over the past decade. He's regularly invited to be a guest speaker, teacher, or workshop presenter at international writing conferences and film festivals worldwide. He hosts an annual writer's retreat in Greece, where he currently lives. He focuses his teaching on how to get tension and emotion in every scene, on every page, how he made it as a creator/writer, the path to success in this business, and the pitfalls to avoid. He also hosts a reading retreat in Greece with guest authors, yoga retreats, and hiking retreats. Visit the Imagine Greece Retreats website at www.imaginegreeceretreats.com, or email him directly to discuss an opportunity to join one of the retreats at jonas@imaginegreeceretreats.com.

Jonas is also a professional freelance editor. He works for several publishers and does private editing for clients, with many testimonials on his website at www.imaginepress.org, which details each author's response to Jonas's editing skills. Email Jonas directly for an editing quote at editor@imaginepress.org.

To book Jonas for a speaking engagement at a writer's conference/festival, to have him on your jury at a film festival, or even to say hello, email Jonas directly at jonassaul@icloud.com.

For updates on releases, hit the "Follow" button on Amazon or Bookbub, and join Jonas on Facebook, where he's most active.

Contact Jonas Saul

Linktree: Find me here

Email: jonassaul@icloud.com

* 9 7 8 1 9 9 8 0 4 7 8 2 6 *